WHILE
THE
OTHERS
SLEEP

Tom Becker won the Waterstone's Children's Book
Prize for his first novel, *Darkside*, aged 25. Born
and brought up in West Lancashire,
he now lives in London.

TOM BECKER
WHILE THE OTHERS SLEEP

First published in the UK in 2013 by Scholastic Children's Books
An imprint of Scholastic Ltd
Euston House, 24 Eversholt Street
London, NW1 1DB, UK
Registered office: Westfield Road, Southam, Warwickshire, CV47 0RA
SCHOLASTIC and associated logos are trademarks and/or
registered trademarks of Scholastic Inc.

Text © Tom Becker, 2013

The right of Tom Becker to be identified as the author
of this work has been asserted by him.

ISBN 978 1 4071 0953 4

A CIP catalogue record for this book
is available from the British Library.

Printed and bound by CPI Group (UK) Ltd, Croydon, CR0 4YY
Papers used by Scholastic Children's Books are made
from wood grown in sustainable forests.

1 3 5 7 9 10 8 6 4 2

This is a work of fiction. Names, characters, places,
incidents and dialogues are products of the author's imagination
or are used fictitiously. Any resemblance to actual people, living
or dead, events or locals is entirely coincidental.

www.scholastic.co.uk/zone

For Lindsay; for the precious gift of peace at midnight,
and bright dreams of tomorrow.

PROLOGUE

A SPARK OF LIGHT

It began with a whisper, a secret shared in the hush of midnight.

It began with the rasp of a match, and a spark of light in the darkness.

It began with a hint of a smile on a child's face.

The floor of the parlour was strewn with torn book pages, which rustled softly as the child knelt down. Slowly, with the solemn tenderness of a mourner laying flowers at a grave, they lowered the fizzing match. There was a crackle as the pages caught, a curling and blackening of sepia. The child's mischievous breath played upon the flame, coaxing it across the paper, and within seconds the fire was spreading across the floor. Bare feet padded out of the room, and the parlour door closed with a satisfied click.

Left alone to plot and scheme, the flames crept along the wooden skirting boards, clambering up curtains and clinging on to the bookshelves. Within minutes the room was choked with smoke. Gathering in rage, the fire erupted from the parlour with a snarl, stalking into the corridor outside and making for the staircase with a dark, violent intent.

The smell of burning carried up to a box-room at the top of the stairs, where a slumbering attendant awoke with a start. He hurriedly buttoned up his shirt and raced out of his room, swearing loudly at the sight of the fire roaring up the stairs. The attendant ran along the landing banging on doors, his cries of alarm drawing the other adults from their rooms. They fled shrieking from the onrushing flames, stumbling and coughing down the backstairs and out into the safe embrace of the night air. There the women broke down and sobbed upon the lawns, while the men watched helplessly as the fire devoured their possessions.

Amid the crackle of flames and groan of timbers, a back door opened in the distant west wing of the building. A host of pale spectres came floating out upon the breeze, small figures in white nightshirts.

They had forgotten about the children.

Biting back oaths, the attendants hurried across the grass and began herding the children away from the house, their gruff barks masking guilt at having left their charges to fend for themselves. At the top of the slope looking out over the lake, the inhabitants of Scarbrook House came together – doctor and patient, adult and child – and watched, united in their bewilderment, as the building's east wing succumbed to the flames.

A hasty summit was called, during which one of the doctors volunteered to cycle down to the local village for help. An argument broke out amongst the men, with several of them pointing fingers at a portly, whiskered man in a nightshirt and sleeping cap.

"Well what on earth would you have me do?" he retorted angrily. "The nearest fire brigade is over twenty miles away in London! Do you think we can put this out with buckets of water? Until the men come from the village there's little we can do but pray that the fire burns itself out."

Whilst the adults argued, the children appeared overwhelmed by the blaze. Some milled around in a daze; others sat down on the grass and picked daisies, singing softly to themselves; others capered gleefully, their faces turning an impish red in the fiery glow. One boy burst into sudden howls of laughter, bending double at some unexplained hilarity until his breaths became wheezes and sobs wracked his body.

There was a loud crash of falling masonry, and a scream rent the night sky. A girl with tumbling black hair broke away from the other children and ran towards the knot of doctors, a tall, good-looking boy on her heels.

"Someone's still inside!" the girl cried. "You have to save them!"

The portly man with the whiskers shook his head. "We've done a full headcount. There's no one in the building."

"But the screams!"

The boy stepped forward and gently grasped her arm. "It's the horses," he said quietly. "The fire's reached the stables."

Another shriek joined the first, then another. The girl paled. She found herself wishing that the flames could burn even louder, and roar with greater ferocity – anything to block out the horses' screams. They were piercing screeches torn from inhuman throats, terrible hymns of searing pain and charred flesh. As the adults listened, grim-faced, some of the children joined in, throwing back their heads to add their own banshee shrieks and wolf howls, filling the air with an unholy chorus of anguish. The dark-haired girl shuddered and turned away, shrugging off her companion's attempts to comfort her.

Away from the others, in the shadows by the entrance to the rock garden, two smaller figures stood in silence. The girl shrank back from the inferno, her face drenched with an unspoken horror. She clutched a rag doll tightly to her chest, burying her face in its hair as the last stricken aria from the stables died away. Beside her the boy watched impassively, his large round eyes betraying no flicker of emotion.

"It's all right," he said soothingly. "There's nothing to fear. The fire can't hurt you now."

As the boy raised his hand to shield his eyes from the glare, he noticed a dark smudge on the end of his fingertip. He carefully brushed the residue away, aware of the telltale scent of a burnt match.

"You just stay close to me," the boy continued, wrapping an arm around the girl. "I'll take care of you."

CHAPTER ONE

BITTER WELCOME

Tick. Tock. Tick. Tock.

The grandfather clock dolorously paced out the silence as Alfie Mandeville waited, hands clasped patiently behind his back. Everywhere he looked around the study there were hints and subtle boasts of wealth and success. Bookcases sagged under the weight of thick medical journals. Plunging leather armchairs looked deep enough to swallow a man whole. A row of crystal wine glasses had been arranged on a bureau in a manner seemingly designed to catch the light, while the ornate gas lamps were grey and dormant in the brilliant summer afternoon. Through the bay windows, the lawns sloped languidly down towards a line of birch trees. Alfie caught a glimpse of himself in one of the panes, and saw a tall, rangy boy with a mop of sandy blond hair staring back at him.

In front of Alfie a man was seated behind a polished desk, peering at a letter through half-moon spectacles. He cut a plump, satisfied figure, the first white flecks of middle age dusting his whiskers like icing sugar. From

5

time to time he broke off to take a slurp of tea from a china cup. The man was taking a long time over the letter – although whether that was because he found its contents pleasing or disturbing was hard to tell. Eventually he put down the piece of paper and loudly cleared his throat.

"Well now," he declared. "There we have it."

"My father has always spoken very highly of you, Dr Grenfell," Alfie said quickly. "He says that if anyone can help me, you can."

"And no man holds Lord Mandeville in greater regard than myself," replied the doctor. "Over the years Scarbrook House has been indebted to his frequent and most generous donations. However. . ." Grenfell trailed off, waving vaguely at the letter.

"Is there a problem, sir?"

"Ordinarily I would do anything in my power to help a Mandeville. But you must understand – the condition your father describes in his letter—"

"Insomnia, I believe they call it."

"Quite, quite. This . . . insomnia . . . does not fall within the compass of our medical programmes. Scarbrook House provides a home for well-bred young gentlemen and ladies with recognized mental conditions: anxiety and nervousness, melancholia, feminine hysteria. I am not sure that mere sleeping problems necessitate admittance."

"My father asks for no guarantees," said Alfie. "Merely that I can stay here for a time under your observation." He hesitated. "He also instructed me to say that he heard about the accident here last month."

Dr Grenfell glanced up sharply. "The fire, you mean?"

"My father says that rebuilding the east wing will cost a great deal of money, and that if he was sure you were taking care of me, he would be glad to help. A token of friendship, he called it."

"A token of friendship," echoed Dr Grenfell, nodding slowly as he sat back in his chair. "I see. Well, then: tell me exactly what the problem is."

Alfie frowned. "Well . . . I can't sleep, sir."

"Quite," the doctor responded, pressing the tips of his fingers together. "Do continue."

"I'm not sure what else I can say," said Alfie. "I can't sleep. It doesn't matter how long I lie in bed, or how tired I am. Morning comes, and I'm still awake."

"How long have you been suffering from this condition?"

Alfie made some quick mental calculations. "Two months?" he ventured. "Three?"

It was hard to be certain. Alfie couldn't remember a precise date, the first time he had lain awake all night. He had had no such problems in India, and even on the Mandevilles' return to London – the biting December wind gnawing on bodies slow-roasted by two years in the heat of Calcutta – Alfie had slept normally. Then, one April or May night, he had been unable to drop off. One sleepless night had become two, then three.

Alfie began to haunt the midnight hallways of the Mandevilles' Chelsea townhouse, pacing up and down the corridors in an attempt to exhaust himself into sleep. All he succeeding in doing was waking up the butler, Stowbridge, who angrily shooed him back to bed.

The toll of these barren nights could be detected in Alfie's bloodshot eyes and the ghostly pallor of his skin. Dark rumours began circulating amongst the servants in the kitchens and pantries of the great London mansions – the young Mandeville slept only in the daytime, he had been seen in a graveyard in the middle of the night, his teeth were as sharp as daggers. . .

Though his parents took no heed of servants' gossip, Alfie knew that he was embarrassing them. He found himself nodding off during the daytime, often at inopportune moments – during a meal with the French Ambassador, he caused cries of alarm when he slumped unconscious into his plate of food. In private, Alfie's father sharply criticized his weary demeanour, whilst his mother patted his hand dreamily and told him to go to bed earlier. Though his parents had never overburdened Alfie with affection or attention, he noticed a slight increase in the distance between them, a new note of shame in their voices when they mentioned his name. Then again, in the lofty circles in which the Mandeville family moved, appearance was everything. They were one of the richest and most important families in the Empire, and Alfie was their only son. Anything that could cause raised eyebrows in a Pall Mall gentleman's club, or wagging tongues at a dinner party in Mayfair, had to be avoided at all costs.

Even so, the decision to send him away took Alfie by surprise with its swiftness. He was sitting up in bed reading, the candles burning low, when Lord Richard Mandeville – the fearless explorer and businessman, the toast of London's aristocracy, the "White Tiger of the Raj" – strode into his bedroom and told him to prepare for travel to Scarbrook. Alfie's protests died in his throat when he saw the look in his father's eye. It was said that even the prime minister thought twice before disagreeing with Lord Mandeville. What chance had a fourteen-year-old boy of changing the White Tiger's mind?

And Scarbrook did have certain things to recommend it. Much to the relief of Alfie's father, the true nature of its medical activities was carefully concealed. To genteel ears, "sanatorium" sounded little better than "asylum" or "madhouse", whereas the casual listener might have mistaken Scarbrook House for a finishing school. And naturally, as one of the institution's most generous benefactors, Lord Mandeville could rely upon an especial amount of discretion.

Preparations for Alfie's departure were carried out with discreet haste, the townhouse's windows burning late into the night as servants hurriedly packed Alfie's bags. Alfie left early the next morning. His hopes of saying farewell to his mother were dashed with the news that she had fallen ill again. Lady Mandeville suffered from recurring spells of lethargy that she called "the shades", which drove her to her bed and left her too fragile to see any visitors. Even as her son's carriage rattled away down the drive, the curtains over Lady Mandeville's bedroom window remained firmly closed. Lord Mandeville had managed a brisk handshake and a pat on the arm, without ever making eye contact with his son. The only consolation of Alfie's hasty departure was the absence of Stowbridge, whose displeasure Alfie feared almost more than his father's.

The carriage fled London through a thick pall of fog, heading for the Hertfordshire countryside. It was well over an hour before the first glimpse of patchwork fields appeared through the grey, and by that time Alfie's eyelids were drooping. A childish melody popped into his head unbidden, a line from a lullaby his mother used to sing to him:

"My lady wind, my lady wind, went round about the house. . ."

As Alfie tried to recall the next line, he was distracted by the sight of the hedgerows whipping past him in a thorny blur. The coachman's lash sounded clear and hard over the rattle of carriage wheels and the horses' whinnied protests. The animals were being driven at a furious pace – surely too quickly for these narrow lanes. The vehicle took a sharp right turn, throwing Alfie against the side of the carriage. He thought about banging on the roof of the carriage and shouting at the coachman to stop, before deciding against it. After all, this would not be a journey that would appeal to a man from his superstitious class – despite the careful curtain Scarbrook House drew around its activities, whispers about its troubled patients still reached the capital. Anyway, Alfie supposed, the sooner the coachman returned to London, the sooner he could get to the alehouse.

He clung on to the door handle as the lane narrowed still further, low-hanging branches clawing at the carriage roof. Then, suddenly, the vehicle exploded between two gateposts and flew along a long gravel driveway coiled up a hillside. Alfie's breath caught in his throat as he gazed out of the window.

Situated directly on the hill's brow, Scarbrook House added a flourish of dark drama to the horizon. It was a sprawling country house consisting of a central block flanked by two arcaded wings, which faced off against one another across a gravel yard. The roofs were a confusion of domes and towers and pointed eaves, giving the building an air at once both haughty and haphazard. A dense wood ran around the back of the house, providing a natural boundary to vast grounds that contained not only a rock garden and a lake, but also a folly built in the style of an Asian pagoda. The estate's motley appearance was accentuated by the fact that Scarbrook's entire eastern wing was a blackened ruin of charred stonework, with an aching hole where its roof should have been.

As the carriage crunched across the gravel yard, the coachman wrenched on his horses' reins, bringing the vehicle to an abrupt halt by the front entrance. He all but threw Alfie's suitcases down from the roof, glancing fearfully at the house before scrambling back into his seat. Alfie's feet had barely touched the ground before the whip had lashed again, and the carriage was hastening back down the hill and out of the grounds. As he picked up the suitcase, Alfie resolved not to tell his father about the coachman's rudeness. He did not believe in telling tales, no matter what the provocation.

Juggling awkwardly with his luggage, he walked up to the front door and rang the bell. A young woman in a black dress and an apron answered. She was disconcertingly beautiful, with large brown eyes set into an oval, dusky face. It was a struggle for Alfie to remember his manners, and not stare at her open-mouthed.

"I'm here to see Dr Grenfell?" Alfie said uncertainly. "He should be expecting me."

If the serving girl was surprised to see him standing alone on the doorstep, she didn't betray it.

"Follow me," she said, a trace of a hot, foreign climate softening the edges of her English accent.

Gesturing Alfie inside the building, she led him through a deserted hallway into a warren of parlours and drawing rooms. The grandeur was tainted by the smell of burned wood that had infected the entire building, leaving an ashy aftertaste in every room. When they arrived by a study door, the girl knocked twice and left Alfie outside, telling him to wait in a tone that didn't invite any further questions.

Presently there came the sound of a throat clearing, and then a voice called Alfie inside. Even Alfie had heard of Dr Edmund Grenfell. One of the most esteemed medical men of his generation, his lectures were applauded in Paris, his journal articles digested and debated in New York, and his teachings followed to the letter in the famous sanatoria outside Geneva. Given his global fame, it was something of a surprise that the doctor had decided to settle in Hertfordshire, dedicating his talents to a handful of young patients. Perhaps Alfie should have felt reassured by the thought of entering Dr Grenfell's care – but in truth he was scared. He had visions of gibbering loons thrashing about in strait-waistcoats, crazed murderers attacking him in his bed. After all, Alfie wasn't *mad*. He just couldn't sleep.

Yet what was the alternative? Lord Mandeville had made it clear that he didn't want his son home until he was cured. There was no way Alfie could return to Chelsea before then, no matter how much he wanted to. He was the sole heir to the Mandeville name and fortune. It was his duty to get well again.

A loud slurp of tea brought Alfie back to the study, and the matter in hand. Dr Grenfell appeared to have come to a decision.

"Well then, Master Mandeville," he declared, folding up the letter and placing it in his desk drawer. "Let's see if there is anything that can be done for you."

CHAPTER TWO

THE MADHOUSE

Dr Grenfell's footsteps echoed around Scarbrook House, a clipped, self-important drumbeat upon the polished wooden floorboards. Alfie had to hurry to keep up with him, and they soon left the aged attendant carrying Alfie's suitcases struggling in their wake. They moved so quickly that the rooms became a glittering blur, studded with tapestries and Turkish rugs, priceless china and antique pistols. Scarbrook House looked more like a stately home or a rajah's palace than a sanatorium. Even the acrid waft of burned wood seemed to have died away.

"Currently we have thirty-two guests staying with us," Dr Grenfell explained in the library, as Alfie peered at the antique map of Europe hanging on the wall. "They are aged between ten and sixteen – when the mind is still impressionable, like clay, and imperfections can be smoothed out by a knowledgeable hand. Younger than ten, and our guests lack the necessary maturity to understand the need for change. Older than sixteen, and the mind becomes hardened, set in its ways. By then,

I fear, all is lost." Dr Grenfell paused. "How old are you, Master Mandeville?" he asked.

"Fourteen," Alfie said quickly.

"Perfect."

The library's sash windows were open, allowing a faint breeze to alleviate the stifling heat inside the room. A group of boys were scampering across the lawns outside, laughing raucously as they played tag.

"This place isn't at all as I'd imagined it," Alfie said cautiously. "People seem quite . . . happy."

"So I should hope, Master Mandeville," replied Dr Grenfell, with evident satisfaction. "It is 1897 – we are at the eve of a new century! Attitudes are changing as quickly as the times. This will be the age of the motor car and the aeroplane. Medicine cannot remain in the dark ages, reliant upon leeches and astrological charts. Would you believe that scarcely thirty, forty years ago, there were great stigmas attached to diseases of the mind? People were shut away in asylums, shackled and locked up in conditions unfit for an animal. Here at Scarbrook House, the objective is not to confine or restrain those in our care. This is not a prison, and our guests are not criminals. They come from the highest circles of our society, and demand to be treated accordingly. Freedom, diet, exercise: that is our mantra. It is forward thinking such as this that makes Scarbrook House the envy of British medicine, and British medicine the envy of the rest of the world!"

The doctor ended his speech on a rousing note, his

finger jabbing towards the ceiling. He left the library with renewed vigour, marching down the long corridor past a stairwell that led down into darkness. As he peered over the edge of the iron railing, Alfie made out a sturdy door at the bottom of the steps.

"What's down here?" he asked.

"No dawdling, please!" replied Dr Grenfell, propelling Alfie away from the stairwell with a firm hand. "Time and tide wait for no man."

He led Alfie into the adjoining drawing room, which owed its sweltering, gloomy air to the thick red drapes drawn across the windows. In the crimson shadows it took Alfie a couple of seconds to realize that the room was filled with girls. They glanced up shyly from their books at the sight of him, giggling and whispering to their friends. A girl with cropped hair erupted into a full-throated crone's cackle, then reddened and clasped a hand to her mouth, as though she had burped. Dr Grenfell shot a warning glance at the unfortunate girl and beckoned Alfie onwards.

"Although Scarbrook House treats both of the sexes," he explained quietly, "we do not encourage overfamiliarity. As a rule of thumb, boys and girls should leave each other alone. There are a lot of fragile temperaments here – we do not want to test them further with any unnecessary ... ah ... stimulation."

They left the girls in the drawing room and walked through into a cavernous hall, which was dominated by a sweeping staircase and a crystal chandelier that unfolded like a sparkling flower bud above their heads. Alfie's eye was drawn to a painting over the hearth on the far wall, in which a white-haired nobleman glowered out over the hall.

"Sir Thomas Scarbrook," Dr Grenfell announced proudly. "Our benevolent patron. He bequeathed this house to our foundation some ten years ago."

"A very generous gesture, sir," Alfie said politely.

Grenfell nodded. "Sir Thomas was a much misunderstood man," he mused. "It is true he possessed a fiery temper, and that old age only increased his impatience. In the last few years of his life he became a recluse, refusing entry to all visitors apart from your father. Sir Thomas never really recovered from the shock of losing his boy Frederick. Such a terrible tragedy, to lose a son so young."

"I have heard my father talk of Frederick Scarbrook," said Alfie. "They were close friends, weren't they?"

"Inseparable!" the doctor responded. "The two of them were famed throughout the colonies as a pair of dashing and adventurous travellers. The accident in Africa left your father inconsolable. In the years following Fred's death Lord Mandeville remained a regular visitor to Hertfordshire, despite Sir Thomas' increasing irascibility. And since the establishment of our institution he has continued to support our efforts, all in the name of his friend." Grenfell glanced down at Alfie. "Lord Mandeville has always had a heightened sense of his responsibilities. It's part of what makes him a great man – and such a great deal to live up to."

"I will do my very best," Alfie replied.

The doctor nodded and ploughed onwards up the grand staircase, to the visible dismay of the attendant, who had only just caught up with them. On the first-floor landing, they turned left and headed down a corridor that led to a large dormitory room.

"And here we have the boys' bedroom," said Dr Grenfell. He pointed towards the bed at the far end of the left-hand wall. "This bed has recently become free. You should find it tolerably comfortable. Tomorrow morning I will discuss your case with my colleagues and decide how we are to proceed. Lord Mandeville can rest assured that Scarbrook House will do everything in its power to help you." He gave Alfie a sideways look. "You will put his mind at ease on that matter, won't you?"

"I shall write to him this evening," Alfie said obligingly.

"Good, good." Dr Grenfell pulled out a fob watch from his waistcoat pocket and consulted the dial. "I'm afraid you've just missed lunch, but dinner is served daily at six o'clock sharp, which gives you the afternoon to unpack. I must leave you – there are other patients demanding my attention."

"Of course," said Alfie. "Thank you very much, sir."

The doctor bustled out of the bedroom with a farewell harrumph, nearly knocking the perspiring attendant off his feet. Left alone in the empty dormitory, surrounded by rows of identical beds, Alfie tried to stop his heart from sinking. Like it or not, this was his home now. A Mandeville made the best of things. Puffing out his cheeks, Alfie opened his suitcases and began transferring his clothing into his wardrobe.

He was kneeling by his bedside cabinet, putting away his writing paper and pens, when his ears caught the sound of faint whispering drifting into the bedroom like a draught from the corridor.

Alfie straightened up. "Hello?" he called out. "Who's there?"

Instantly his mind conjured nightmarish visions of axe-wielding killers, but when the door opened it revealed only boyish faces peering curiously in his direction. Their owners trailed slowly, almost shyly, into the bedroom, out of breath and with their sleeves rolled up. It was the boys Alfie had seen playing outside.

"Hello there," he said, with a relieved smile.

"We heard a rumour you were coming," a young voice piped up.

"You're a Mandeville?" another said disbelievingly.

Alfie nodded. "Word travels quickly around here."

"There isn't a great deal to talk about." The speaker was both the tallest boy and the oldest-looking. He had to be a couple of years older than Alfie, with jet-black hair that flicked down over his eyes and sharp, prominent cheekbones. He was coolly handsome, and seemingly well aware of that fact.

"He's got Harker's bed!" a smaller boy whispered,

earning himself a nudge in the ribs from the dark-haired boy.

"Not now, Brooke," he said. Tucking the lock of hair behind his ear, the boy stepped forward and offered Alfie his hand. "William Travers," he said, a devilish smile playing on his lips. "Welcome to the Madhouse."

Several hours later, scrubbed clean and changed for dinner, the patients presented themselves in the dining room for the evening meal. A group of doctors occupied the top table with Edmund Grenfell, a small but merry band whose enjoyment of the meal increased with every top-up of wine and port. Travers insisted that Alfie sit next to him, and the elder boy quickly proved a goldmine of gossip and scandal. He spent the meal pointing other patients out to Alfie, and quietly outlining their various afflictions:

"Sampson's in line to be the next Earl of Winchester, only he can't stop wetting the bed – and at fifteen, too! His father can barely look him in the eye. The boy next to Sampson is Rothermere, who seems like a nice enough fellow but flies into hideous rages at the drop of a hat. I presume that Brooke is here merely on account of him being such an insufferable sap. But the boys are nothing compared to the girls. Lucy Albright refuses to eat, Constance Cherwell has violent fits, and as for Sophie Wetherby. . ." His voice dropped to a whisper. "They say she likes other girls."

Alfie's eyes widened disbelievingly.

"And you see that girl over there?" Travers nodded towards a pretty blonde at the next table. "Daughter of the Marquis of Salisbury, and a very pleasant-looking thing to boot, but stay well clear. She had her embroidery kit confiscated after threatening to take out a nurse's eye with a needle."

"How awful!" gasped Alfie. "You'd never guess looking at her. She doesn't look ill at all!"

Travers burst out laughing. "No one here's actually *ill*, Alfie. Old Doc Grenfell would rather eat nettles than use that word. We're not patients, we're guests. We're too rich to be *mad*."

"Shh!" a red-headed boy said indignantly across the table. "You can't say that!"

"I'll say what I damn well like, Perkins," Travers shot back, his voice suddenly hard as flint. "And unless you want to feel my fist in your face, you won't disagree with me."

Travers' gaze was furious, and he was gripping his knife so tightly that the knuckles on his right hand had turned white. Hastily Perkins mumbled an apology and returned to his dinner.

"Anyway," Travers continued to Alfie, his airy demeanour restored, "what brings you here? What dreadful secret are you hiding?"

"Insomnia."

Travers raised an eyebrow. "Can't sleep, eh? Doesn't sound too awful to me."

"You're not a Mandeville," Alfie replied gloomily.

"Well, fear not," Travers declared, clapping him on the back. "Such an esteemed name requires some kind of manservant, and I'd be more than happy to oblige. After all, my father's only a measly old merchant."

Alfie blinked. The Travers Trading Company was known around the world for its dealings in the East Indies. Its spice empire had made John Travers one of the wealthiest men in the Empire – hardly a measly old merchant. Alfie wondered what particular ailment had brought William to Scarbrook. Although Travers seemed happy enough sharing the other patients' maladies, he offered no clue to his own.

As he mopped up the dregs of his stew with a piece of bread, Alfie noticed two younger patients sitting alone at the far end of the table. A sallow-faced boy was hunched over his meal, rocking slightly, whilst a girl stared dolefully into space, her meal untouched. A small porcelain doll rested on the table by her plate.

"Who are they?" Alfie asked.

Travers' face darkened. "That's Yardley and his sister Catherine. Yardley makes the rest of us look downright normal. He tells anyone who'll listen to him that he receives messages from the spirit world."

"The spirit world?"

"I *did* tell you he was a nutcase. Wait until you hear the whole story. A year ago he warns his parents – Lord and Lady Derbyshire to you and me – that they're in terrible danger, and that they have to leave their home immediately. Of course, not being insane, the Lord and

Lady tell him not to be so stupid. Only a week later, they're dead."

"Yardley was right?"

"Of course he was right!" laughed Travers. "He was the one who did them in. He burned down their house in the middle of the night."

Alfie gasped.

"Well, quite. Yardley's uncle had a devil of a job keeping it quiet – had to pretend it was an accident. He said that Yardley and Catherine had also died in the fire, even staged their own funerals. Secretly he sent them to Scarbrook and gave Grenfell an *obscene* amount of money to make sure they stay here."

Alfie frowned. "But if it was Yardley who started the fire, why is Catherine here? What did she do?"

"You'd have to ask her," Travers replied slyly. "Don't expect much of a reply, though. She's mute."

The tale fascinated and repelled Alfie in equal measure. He glanced again at the brother and sister. Although there was no denying that Yardley looked odd, Alfie found it hard to credit that such a small boy could have committed such a dreadful deed. A sudden thought occurred to him.

"So do you think it might have been Yardley who set fire to Scarbrook?" he asked.

"Of course it was him!" Travers exclaimed. "The boy's obsessed with fire! He's not allowed to keep a matchbox or candles by his bedside, and our matches get counted every morning to check none have been stolen."

"Then why hasn't Yardley been taken away?"

Travers leaned in closer. "Because even though we all know he's guilty, none of us can prove it. The attendants went through his things but couldn't find anything linking him to the fire. Old Grenfell's proving unusually firm on the point – keeps muttering about 'fairness' and 'British justice', the batty old quack."

"They should search the grounds," Alfie declared. "He could have buried the evidence – a matchbox stolen from the kitchens, or a rag soaked in oil, perhaps."

"You sound quite the sleuth, Lord Mandeville," grinned Travers. "Mr Arthur Conan Doyle would be proud of you."

"Arthur who?" Alfie asked.

Travers rolled his eyes.

After they had polished off a pudding of rhubarb crumble, the patients went through to the library, where Edmund Grenfell – clearly fancying himself a dramatic orator – read them passages from Milton's *Paradise Lost*. The doctor was slurring his words, and his hands were unsteady as they turned the pages. Alfie wondered whether he had enjoyed one glass of wine too many with his meal. Beside him Travers had to fake a coughing fit to mask his sniggers.

Night had fallen by the reading's end, and the patients climbed the staircase to their bedrooms through the lamplight's gentle glow. They separated on the landing, heading in opposite directions towards the boys' and girls' bedrooms. Alfie's long journey to Scarbrook was resting heavily on his bones, and he wondered whether he might fall asleep that night. He hoped so; the sooner he started sleeping normally, the sooner he could go home.

"Do you see the fire?"

Alfie turned around to find Yardley looking at him. There were still chunks of stew daubed around the boy's mouth, and his cheek was streaked with dirt. His expression was one of intense seriousness.

"I'm sorry," Alfie said politely. "I don't know what you mean. What fire?"

"The fire that awaits. I see it, as bright and clear as if it were burning now." Yardley grabbed Alfie by the arm, jagged fingernails digging into his flesh. "You have to get out of here," he urged. "Before it's too late!"

"Get off me!" cried Alfie, trying to shake himself free. Yardley stared at him, his eyes wide with meaning as he tightened his grip. Finally Travers intervened, stepping in and peeling Yardley's fingers from Alfie's arm.

"Go and annoy someone else," he said, clipping Yardley hard around the head. Yardley howled with pain and scuttled off into the dormitory, where he dived into bed and yanked the blanket up to his eyeballs.

"See what I mean?" Travers said to Alfie. "Absolute lunatic."

Alfie followed him into the dormitory, rubbing his sore arm. The room settled into an agreeable hubbub as the boys prepared for bedtime, changing into nightshirts and brushing their teeth. Alfie wrote a brief letter to his father, informing him that he had arrived safely, and taking care to stress Dr Grenfell's helpfulness. He was signing off when an attendant came round to announce lights out, checking that the boys were in bed before turning out the gas lamps.

Just before the last light was extinguished and the room was swallowed up in darkness, Alfie glanced over at Yardley's bed. The boy was watching him from the other side of the room, his gaze as insistent as the fingers that had gripped Alfie's arm.

CHAPTER THREE

SELENA

Quickly realizing that his hopes of sleep that night were forlorn, Alfie resigned himself to the long wait until morning. He had become so accustomed to not sleeping that he had stopped trying, and his eyes remained wide open for hours, tracing the outlines of the beds and the other boys in the darkness. The bedroom was shrouded in a thick hush only occasionally disturbed by a whimper or a snivel, or a squeak of breaking wind.

As the darkness ceded to a smudged grey dawn, there was a creak from the bed next to him, and Travers rose quietly from his bed. Alfie watched as the dark-haired boy carefully poured water from a jug into a metal bowl and washed his face and hands. After glancing quickly around the room, Travers picked up a small shaving mirror, lifted up his nightshirt and inspected his side. Alfie was shocked to see a latticework of scars covering the boy's skin, angry red ravines that ran from his spine to his belly button.

With a start, Alfie realized that Travers was watching him in his shaving mirror.

"Keep your eyes to yourself, Mandeville," Travers said coldly.

"S-sorry," Alfie stammered, the boy's gaze pinning him to the bedsheets. Travers stared at him for several seconds before putting down the mirror and letting go of his nightshirt. When he spoke again, Travers' voice had regained an even tone.

"Sleep well?"

"No," replied Alfie.

Travers snorted. "I suppose you wouldn't be here if you had, would you?"

Alfie reluctantly swung his legs out of bed and got up, washing in his own bowl and climbing into his clothes. Even though the morning was still in its infancy, it was already warm – by noon Alfie fancied it would be stifling.

After breakfast, an attendant delivered Alfie a summons to meet Dr Grenfell in the auditorium. The attendants were the worker bees of Scarbrook's hive: part orderlies, part nurses, part jail keepers. They dressed sombrely, in rainy hues – the men in heavy grey suits and waistcoats, with matching peaked caps; the women in black dresses buttoned tightly to the neck, their hair pinned up beneath an off-white hat. The men sported facial hair of varying lengths and wildness, from slyly clipped moustaches to tangled hedgerow beards, while the women were as clean and brisk as a scrubbing brush. Their duties were strictly divided along gender lines: women dealt with the girls, men the boys. Although the attendants were grudgingly polite to the patients, Alfie had the feeling that they silently noted down every strange incident in order to tell it later around the kitchen table or in the village pub – as a joke or a horror story, depending upon the material. For their part, most of the patients tended to view the attendants as little more than menial servants. The exception was William Travers, who knew all the men by name and spoke to them with a respectful ease that was generally reciprocated, whilst he alone could winkle a smile out of the severest attendant.

The auditorium was a large circular room situated at the back of the east wing. Sunlight streamed in through windows set high above a sloped, curving bank of benches. Entering through a side door, Alfie found Dr Grenfell standing at the front of the auditorium, arranging a set of medical instruments on the table before him.

"Ah, Master Mandeville! Come in, come in!"

Alfie had barely taken two steps before the doctor broke into loud verse that reverberated around the auditorium:

"Tired Nature's sweet restorer, balmy sleep!
He, like the world, his ready visit pays,
Where fortune smiles; the wretched he forsakes."

Dr Grenfell smiled at the bemused Alfie. "Edward Young," he explained. "The poet?"

"Oh," Alfie said politely.

"Oh, indeed," the doctor agreed. "Though of course, as a medical man, I do not subscribe to the emotional judgements of the poet. I believe in science, and fact. The facts of science, if you will."

Dr Grenfell opened a burnished wooden case, pulling out a long black stethoscope and plugging the earpieces into his ears.

"Now, if you please," he said, blowing on the chestpiece, "take off your shirt."

As Dr Grenfell pressed the cold stethoscope against his chest, Alfie could smell the sickly morning-after aroma of wine upon the doctor's breath. He sat patiently through a lengthy examination that involved a great deal of weighing and measuring and poking and prodding. Two other doctors appeared to take notes, making Alfie feel like an unwilling actor pushed on to the stage, or some fantastical exhibit at the London Zoo – a giraffe, say, or a polar bear. Dr Grenfell punctuated his measurements with ums and ahs, pursing his lips as he jotted down his findings into a leather-bound notebook. When he had eventually finished, the doctor returned the stethoscope to its box with a watchfulness that reminded Alfie of the snake charmers he had seen in the bazaars of Calcutta.

"As I suspected," Grenfell said thoughtfully. "A complete absence of any physical malady. Brush those bags from your eyes and add a dash of colour to those cheeks, and you'd be a picture of health. Have you been subject to any recent psychological traumas or sudden shocks?"

Alfie thought carefully for a moment before shaking his head.

"As I have already explained," said Dr Grenfell, "I have no personal experience in treating insomnia, but I have taken the liberty of reading up on the subject. There have been great advances in the treatment of sleeplessness, especially in the use of chemical restoratives: potassium bromide, suphonal, chloral hydrate. And, of course, there is always laudanum. But in my opinion reliance upon such chemicals encourages laxity and laziness in equal measure, especially in the young. So instead. . ." Dr Grenfell snapped the stethoscope box shut.

"Long walks!" he declared, with a flourish. "Constitutionals! Cold baths! Forgive my bluntness, but you have an unhealthy pallor, Master Mandeville. The fresh air of the Hertfordshire countryside will do you the power of good. After all, *Mens sana in corpore sano*."

Alfie nodded enthusiastically, waiting for more.

"That will be all."

"Oh." Alfie hurriedly buttoned up his shirt. "Right. Thank you."

He trudged out of the auditorium, leaving the doctors huddled together in deep discussion. Alfie didn't know what to make of his examination. Although he was relieved that Dr Grenfell hadn't prescribed any drugs, especially laudanum, he had been hoping for a little more in the way of treatment.

In the corridor outside, two figures were standing together in an alcove. William Travers was leaning lazily against the wall, whispering into a young female attendant's ear as he stroked her cheek. The girl sprang back at the sound of Alfie's approach, revealing the beautiful face that had greeted him at the entrance to Scarbrook the previous day. When Travers looked up, a flash of anger softened into a dawning smile of recognition.

"My Lord Mandeville!" he said, sketching out an exaggerated bow. "Your faithful servant W. Travers has been anxiously waiting to hear news of your encounter with the esteemed Dr Grenfell. The good lady Maria has been kind enough to keep me company."

Maria blushed, lowering her eyes. "Nice to see you again, sir," she murmured to Alfie.

"So what news?" Travers asked excitedly. "Any dreadful ailments diagnosed? Any dastardly concoctions prescribed?"

"Nothing of the sort," Alfie replied. "Cold baths and long walks."

"That's it?" Travers' face fell. "Barely worth the carriage journey out here. And they call this progress. Still, I've got just the tonic to cheer you up." With a sly grin, he held up a bottle of dark port. "At my request Maria has been kind enough to purloin this from the good doctor's extensive private collection. What do you say we treat ourselves to a little nip?"

Maria's eyes widened with alarm. "William! You said you wouldn't tell anyone!"

"Come, come," replied Travers. "It's not as though Grenfell is going to miss it." He winked at Alfie and mimed lifting up a glass. "The esteemed doctor has more than enough of his own personal medication, if you catch my meaning."

"I don't know, Travers," Alfie said doubtfully.

"Oh, don't be such a bore!" said Travers. "The Mandevilles are world-renowned for their courage and daring. It would be most disappointing to find that you are an imposter or a charlatan. You *are* a Mandeville, aren't you?"

"There's no need to be rude," Alfie said stiffly. "All right, I'll come with you."

"Capital!" beamed Travers. "Then let us away!"

He grabbed Maria by the hand and raced along the corridor and down the back stairs, the pair of them laughing breathlessly. Alfie followed behind, a dubious shadow. It was only his second day at Scarbrook and the last thing he wanted was to get into trouble. His father was disappointed enough with him as things were. But there was something magnetic about William Travers, a promise of gleeful fun and a damning of the consequences that made disagreeing with him seem somehow churlish.

They slipped out of the building and across the lawn, Travers careful to hide his booty from inquisitive eyes. He waited until they were in the safety of the wood beyond before opening the port and taking a deep gulp. They flitted through the sun-dappled trees, taking it in turns to swig from the bottle. The alcohol was strong and sweet, burning Alfie's throat as it slipped down. He soon felt light-headed and giddy, and the sight of Travers capering around made him laugh until his sides ached.

The ground began to slope upwards, and as they climbed, glimpses of a building became apparent through the birches. On Travers' insistence they made towards it, finally coming out into a clearing at the top of the hill. In the middle of the clearing was a hexagonal red-brick tower with a tall chimney running up one of its faces. It was a grim, ugly building that looked no less sullen for its drenching in sunshine.

"What's that?" asked Alfie.

"The water tower," Travers replied. He grinned. "I dare you to go inside and take a look around."

"Why? It's just a water tower."

"Then you won't mind going inside."

"But I don't want to go inside!"

"Scared, are we?"

"Of course not! I just don't—"

"Listen!" Maria hissed suddenly. "Something's coming!"

The sound of rumbling wheels and hooves was fast approaching on the path leading up the other side of the hill. Travers pushed Alfie and Maria back into the trees, ducking down behind a log just as a carriage emerged into the clearing and halted by the front of the water tower.

"The plot thickens," murmured Travers.

Alfie poked his head up above the log. A serving woman hastened down from the vehicle and opened the door, allowing a delicate young woman in a cloak to climb down. As he gazed into the deep folds of the hood, Alfie caught a glimpse of a porcelain female face with haunted, hazel eyes.

"Selena!" he gasped. "Selena Marbury!"

"Selena Marbury?" echoed Travers. "As in, daughter of Lord Richard Marbury? The Viceroy of India?"

Alfie nodded. "We were friends in Calcutta. I'd recognize her anywhere."

"I'm not surprised," said Travers. "By repute she's the prettiest girl in the Empire."

He winced as Maria jabbed a sharp elbow into his ribs. Alfie ignored them. At the sight of Selena's face, the wood had melted away, and he was back in the Mandevilles' home in the Indian capital, comforted by the drowsy wafts of the *punkah* fans above his head and the good-natured scoldings of the *ayahs* as they fussed over him; outside on the verandah, his father had returned from the Bombay Club and was deep in conversation with Stowbridge, the men's faces furrowed in thought.

As the carriage executed a tight turn and rattled away back down the path, the serving woman ushered Selena inside the water tower. The two women disappeared into the building, and the door closed firmly behind them.

"I'd heard she was returning to England several months ago," Alfie said distantly.

"England's one thing," Travers muttered, "but what in God's name is she doing *here*?" He turned to Maria and stroked her cajolingly on the elbow. "I'll wager you know, don't you, sweetheart? Why don't you tell us what the Viceroy's daughter is doing creeping around the grounds of a Hertfordshire nuthouse?"

"I shouldn't say," Maria said quietly.

"You heard Alfie – he's friends with the girl. Isn't it natural, and indeed right, that he should know what's going on?"

Alfie could tell that Maria knew she should keep quiet, but the port had loosened her tongue, and she was clearly enjoying knowing something that Travers didn't. Leaning forward, she whispered: "They say Miss Marbury suffers from violent mood swings when she becomes uncontrollable. She locked herself in her room and tore all her clothes to ribbons; a poor servant girl had her face clawed for coughing whilst Miss Marbury was reading. Then she ruined one of her father's banquets by throwing a drink in his face and smashing glass everywhere. The Viceroy had to remove her from India in disgrace."

"What?" Alfie's jaw dropped open. "Are you sure? That doesn't sound like Selena at all."

"Her father has had her examined by the finest doctors in Harley Street," Maria told him. "They suspect the poor girl is hysterical."

36

"But why the water tower?" asked Alfie. "Why not Scarbrook House with everyone else?"

"No one's supposed to see her. Dr Grenfell's express orders."

"But that's ridiculous!" Alfie protested. "I know her!"

"That's precisely the point," interjected Travers. "None of Scarbrook House's patients are supposed to have had any prior contact with one another. Apparently it increases the risk of contagion. Grenfell's breaking the rules here. I'm sure that the fact that the Viceroy is one of the handful of Englishmen whose wealth compares to your father's has nothing to do with it. With you and Selena here, I imagine Grenfell can build a new east wing *and* treat himself to a few celebratory bottles on the side."

"You shouldn't say such things about the doctor," Maria said disapprovingly. "It's cruel."

"Oh, please accept my apology, Lady Maria!" replied Travers, with an unpleasant sneer. "Have I offended you? I didn't realize you were so delicate. Brushing shoulders with Scarbrook House's noble guests has clearly improved you. After all, before your beloved Dr Grenfell took pity on you and gave you employment, you were nothing more than a petty thief."

Maria flinched, as though she had been struck in the face. "Please, William," she said, an imploring note in her voice. "Don't."

"And look how you repay him," Travers continued

mercilessly, "stealing port from under his very nose. Was this compulsion to thieve drummed into you in the workhouse, or does your Spanish blood mean it comes naturally?"

"You devil!" Maria screamed. She hurled the bottle of port at Travers, narrowly missing both him and Alfie as it smashed against the log. Picking up the hem of her skirt, Maria fled away down the hill, her long black hair bouncing angrily against her back.

"That was unfair, Travers," Alfie remarked. "You asked her to steal the port."

The elder boy waved a hand dismissively. "She's nothing. A common criminal. She should be grateful she's not still walking down Piccadilly trading her virtue for pennies." He barked with laughter at Alfie's shocked expression. "Your gentleman's sensibilities do you credit, My Lord, but a word of advice from the unworthy: don't ever confuse a servant's apron for a nun's habit."

Travers squatted down and began picking up fragments of the broken port bottle. "Better remove the evidence, hadn't we? Don't want old Sherlock Grenfell— Ow! Damn it!" He plucked a shard of glass from a jagged, bloody wound in his palm. "Typical. Clumsy Travers strikes again. . . Now then, what's wrong with you?"

Alfie was bent double, clutching at his stomach as he retched. He couldn't stand the sight of blood. As a young boy he had stumbled across the splattered remnants of a blackbird in the grounds of the Mandeville's country house. It had been attacked by a fox – its innards torn from its breast, spilling out across the grass. It was an image Alfie had never been able to shake off, haunting the back of his mind like the ghost in a spirit photograph.

"It's the blood," he gasped. "Makes me sick."

"Here, it's all right. Look!" Travers wrapped a handkerchief around his palm, staunching the wound. "Like it never happened."

Alfie wiped the back of his hand across his mouth and took several deep breaths. "Sorry. I can't help it. Just looking at it. . ."

"You are a veritable bundle of nerves," Travers said critically. "No wonder you can't sleep! Let us get out of here and adjourn to the games room. I have just taught Rothermere how to play rummy, and he is rich and stupid in equal measure. You'll feel better with a few coins jangling in your pockets."

Numbly, Alfie allowed Travers to lead him down the hill, not looking back at the water tower as it disappeared behind the trees, hiding Selena Marbury from view.

CHAPTER FOUR

A MEAGRE CONGREGATION

On returning to Scarbrook, Alfie politely rebuffed Travers' invitation to play cards and went to the library to read instead. Lord Mandeville declared gambling to be the last resort of the weak and sinful, and Alfie didn't want to pick up any bad habits. Besides, Travers' argument with Maria had left a sour taste in his mouth, and the port's aftermath was threatening a headache.

At dinner Alfie pushed his food around on his plate as conversations ricocheted around the table. Judging by Travers' satisfied grin, the card game had ended as he had predicted, but his opponent had taken his losses with good grace. Given the size of Silas Rothermere, that was no bad thing. Rothermere was a broad-shouldered giant with a round, open face and tufted hair like a hatchling. Although he wasn't the quickest of wits, Alfie liked him immediately, and found it hard to believe that such a gentle soul had been sent to Scarbrook on account of his temper. Perhaps Travers had been joking about that. After all, if anyone at Scarbrook seemed to have a problem controlling their temper, it was William Travers himself.

To everyone's relief, there were no poetry readings that evening, and the patients were free to go up to their dormitories early. Perhaps it was the lingering effect of the port, or the cumulative effect of months without proper sleep, but as Alfie settled into bed his eyelids felt heavy, and his mind unusually calm. The giggles and whispers from the other beds were as soothing as waves on a shoreline. . .

Had he fallen asleep? It was hard to be sure. There was the vague sensation of time having passed, and Alfie's thoughts oozed drowsily through his head like syrup. Something must have woken him. Alfie was about to roll over and try to go back to sleep when he realized what had urged him back to consciousness.

Soft, shallow breaths; a presence at his bedside. Someone was standing over him.

Alfie knew that he should call out, but he was too frightened to even open his eyes. He sensed that the figure was almost within touching distance, but it neither moved nor spoke. All it did was watch, and breathe.

He could bear it no longer. Alfie dived over to his bedside table, scrabbled for a match in the box and struck it into life. His surroundings emerged from the darkness, revealing Perkins standing over his bed. Although the redhead's eyes were wide open, his gaze was vacant as he stared down at Alfie.

"For God's sake, Perkins!" hissed Alfie, lighting his bedside candle. "You scared the life out of me! What is it?"

Perkins ignored the question, walking over to Alfie's wardrobe and opening it. Wooden hangers rattled like chattering teeth as he rummaged through the clothes, rousing the other boys from their slumbers. They sat up in their beds, messy haired, squinting into the light, as Perkins selected a bowler hat from the wardrobe and set it with silent satisfaction upon his head.

"Not again!" one boy groaned.

"What's Perkins up to this time?" asked another.

"Looks like he's going for a walk."

"At this time of night?"

"It's not safe!" a third voice quailed. "He should return to bed!"

"Shut up, Yardley," the first boy retorted. "No one asked you."

"We have to do *something*," a new voice insisted primly. "Shall I wake an attendant?"

He was answered by a growl from the bed next to Alfie. "Don't be such a wet, Brooke," Travers muttered, his voice thick with sleep. "If Perkins is sleepwalking again, just bloody well wake him up."

"We can't do that!" protested Brooke. "It's dangerous!"

"It'll be even more dangerous if he trips down the stairs and breaks his neck," replied Travers. "Look, he's already halfway out of the door. PERKINS!"

Perkins jumped in the air with a shocked cry. He gripped hold of the door frame to steady himself and looked fretfully around the dormitory.

"What's happening?" he asked, tears of confusion gathering in his eyes. "Where am I?"

"No need for waterworks, Perkins," Travers said firmly. "You've been on one of your night-time rambles again, that's all. Now take off Alfie's hat and go back to bed."

The shaken Perkins did as he was told. Within minutes, peace reigned in the dormitory once more, and all its occupants were fast asleep – save one. For Alfie, a fragile spell had been broken, a lullaby interrupted, and he was once again wide awake to witness the dawn's creeping entrance.

Later that morning, having trekked over to the folly bathhouse for one of his daily cold baths, Alfie returned to the dormitory to find Travers changing into a dark suit in front of a wardrobe mirror. The older boy had slicked down his locks and looked more dashing than ever – a model of respectability, every inch the wealthy merchant's son.

"You're looking very smart," Alfie said admiringly. "What's the occasion?"

"Funeral," replied Travers, looping a tie around his neck and briskly fastening it into place.

"I'm sorry to hear that," said Alfie. "A relative?"

"Patient. Harker."

The name sounded familiar. Alfie frowned. "Wasn't that the boy who had my bed before me?"

Travers nodded. "Don't worry, though. Maria got most of the bloodstains out."

It took Alfie a few seconds to realize it was a joke. "You're not half as funny as you think you are, you know," he said.

"Quite possibly not," Travers admitted, turning down his shirt collar. He glanced at Alfie in the mirror, scratching his cheek thoughtfully. "Why don't you come along with me?"

"I don't know if I should. . ." Alfie said uncertainly. "I never even met Harker."

"I barely exchanged two words with the poor wretch," said Travers. "But when you've spent as much time inside Scarbrook as I have, you'll seize any opportunity to get out." He consulted his pocket watch. "Better hurry if you're coming, though. I doubt Grenfell will be waiting long today."

Alfie couldn't say why he hurriedly changed into a suit and followed Travers downstairs. Perhaps he felt some sort of unspoken connection with the boy who had slept in his bed, and thus a need to express his condolences. Or perhaps the atmosphere at Scarbrook merely encouraged the ghoulish desire to wallow in sorrow and death.

A meagre congregation, huddled in the shelter of a carriage, awaited them outside. A strong wind was gusting in from the east, teasing the skittish horses and threatening to make off with the mourners' hats. Dr Grenfell was present, alongside a miserable-looking attendant, and a couple of boys Alfie didn't recognize, and also – lingering in the doorway – the unexpected

44

figure of Yardley. The boy's shirt was spilling out over his belt, and his untied shoelaces straggled across the gravel like spiders' legs. Yardley was alone, his mute sister Catherine nowhere to be seen.

The other patients looked surprised when Alfie and Travers appeared, but no one said anything as they joined the party. They left immediately, the attendant climbing up to sit beside the coachman while the boys squeezed next to the doctor inside the carriage. Alfie had been expecting a proper funeral, with a hearse decked out in wreaths and ribbons, and a slow procession following behind it all the way from Scarbrook House to the church. Instead the mourning party galloped away out of the grounds with the grim haste of thieves absconding with the silverware.

The carriage hastened through the winding country lanes, the fields soon giving way to Almsworth, a sleepy village that was little more than a handful of houses clustered around a green. The patients were banned from visiting Almsworth, despite the lure of Sunday cricket matches and the sweet jars in the local shop. Supposedly this was to protect them from any contact with what Grenfell called "unsuitable influences", although the more worldly of Scarbrook's inhabitants knew that this rule was to stop *them* from frightening the villagers.

Using a spindly spire behind the houses as a guide, the carriage clattered past the green and up a sloping road before pulling up outside the front gate of the church.

Grenfell chivvied the mourners out of the vehicle and led them through the grounds, skirting around the side of the church and into the cemetery.

There was an eerie beauty to the scene before them. Beyond the dry stone walls that marked the edge of the graveyard, the ground fell away into rolling hillsides, providing a sweeping backdrop to the black headstones jutting into the view like rotten teeth. The wind lashed the exposed hillside like a cat-o'-nine-tails. Harker's coffin had already been lowered into a hole towards the rear of the graveyard, beneath a plain headstone bearing only his name and the dates of his birth and death. A vicar was standing by its side, while an elderly gravedigger skulked in the background, shaking his head and muttering to himself.

As he approached Harker's final resting place, Alfie noticed the fresh flowers on the neighbouring plot. It was a contrastingly ornate affair, with a marble headstone and small golden bell fitted into a black housing. Alfie had read about such bells in one of his penny dreadfuls, a Gothic serial he had religiously collected from part one to its grisly final instalment. The bells were attached to a line that ran through the earth and down into the coffin, enabling its occupant to ring for help should they wake up to find themselves buried alive. As the mourners formed a slender crescent around Harker's grave, Alfie shivered, and tried to put such gruesome thoughts from his mind.

He nudged Travers. "Where are Harker's family?"

"They won't be coming. Given the circumstances, I'm amazed anyone's here at all."

"What do you mean?"

Travers shrugged. "Harker killed himself, Alfie. I found him swinging from a rope in the woods."

Alfie gasped. "Travers! That's horrible!"

"I suppose."

"But don't his parents want to say farewell?"

"I doubt it. They're probably grateful he's gone." There was a bitterness to Travers' hushed tone. "Don't you understand? We're embarrassments to our families: shameful secrets, illegitimate children. I've been stuck in this godforsaken place for over a year, and do you know how many times my parents have come to visit? Not bloody once."

"Perhaps they're put off by the long journey?"

"We're in Hertfordshire, not darkest Africa!" Travers made a frustrated sound. "There's no talking sense to you sometimes."

Aware that his friend's mood had turned, Alfie fell silent. He was grateful when the vicar stepped forward and indicated that Edmund Grenfell was going to say a few words. The doctor stroked his walrus moustache, deep in thought, and there was a long delay before he spoke.

"I am a man of medicine," he said finally, his voice echoing around the graveyard. "My whole life has been dedicated to the tender care and ministration of the sick and the unfortunate. Compassion runs through my veins." Grenfell paused, before continuing in a rising voice: "But I stand before this wretched handful of mourners to tell you all that I will not pity Richard Harker – not for his brief life, nor for his tragic, misguided end. My heart has no room for the willfully foolish, my eyes no tears for the selfish and the supine. This death – this pitiful *acquiescence* – will lay no claim upon my affections, which will continue to be doled out only to those children with sufficient grace and fortitude to keep faith with their treatment."

His face reddening with anger, Grenfell turned his back on the graveside and walked several paces away. The vicar nodded quickly towards the gravedigger, who came reluctantly forward with his shovel. A shocked silence was punctuated by the thud of earth upon the coffin, and the keening of the wind through the gravestones.

"Not much of a eulogy," whispered Alfie.

"Grenfell's furious," Travers replied. "Suicide's bad for business, and he's got a nasty reputation for losing patients that way. Why do you think he's here, and not in London or New York? He's just lucky that Harker's father is only a civil servant, and not someone actually important."

The wind ruffled the mourners' hair as they watched the coffin vanish beneath a blanket of dirt. Alfie chewed his lip, wishing that the gravedigger would hurry up so that they could leave this bleak cemetery. It didn't help that the man had frozen, his shovel in mid-air. . .

It was then that Alfie's ears caught a gentle tinkling

sound on the breeze. The colour drained from the gravedigger's face, turning it a ghastly shade of pale. Following the man's horrified gaze, Alfie looked round to the neighbouring grave, and saw that the bell above the headstone had started ringing.

The vicar's hand flew to his mouth.

"In the name of all that's holy!" he breathed.

"What's the matter?" snapped Dr Grenfell. "It's only the wind."

"Impossible! The housing around the bell prevents it!" the vicar replied. "Whoever's in that coffin must be alive – we have to dig them out!"

"Are you out of your mind, sir?" As the bell continued to ring, Grenfell grabbed the vicar's arm and pointed a finger towards the headstone. "Read the inscription – this coffin's been buried for five years. Do you think its occupant has just awoken?"

"Then what *is* ringing the bell?" the vicar whispered.

"The dead are disturbed!" the gravedigger moaned. "They sense an intruder! The boy is cursed!"

"I knew I should never have accepted your money!" the vicar hissed at Grenfell. "The presence of this suicide is a stain upon a holy place."

"Rot and nonsense, man!" the doctor thundered back. "Don't be so superstitious! You may finish the ceremony without us."

Clapping his hands together, he ushered the open-mouthed mourners away from Harker's grave. They half stumbled, half ran through the cemetery headstones, pursued all the while by a mocking tinkle that fell silent only as they bundled into the waiting carriage and slammed the door shut behind them. Even then, Alfie swore he could hear the echo of a high-pitched ringing long after they had fled Almsworth.

They travelled back to Scarbrook in silence. Upon arriving, Grenfell stormed off to his study, where he closed the door and didn't emerge for the rest of the day. Alfie waited for Travers to make some kind of smart remark about drinking, but his friend was unusually quiet. Of all the mourners from Harker's graveside, only Yardley appeared unaffected, bidding farewell to the others with an expression on his face that Alfie felt was akin to satisfaction.

CHAPTER FIVE

THE LADY OF THE LAKE

As July ripened into August, the summer laid siege to Scarbrook House, battering its walls with waves of stifling heat and scorching the lawns until they turned parched and brown. Within the sanatorium, the halls and dormitories were steeped in lethargy; voices dropped to a murmur, gestures became vague and uncertain.

Undeterred by the heat, Alfie continued to follow Dr Grenfell's regime of freezing cold baths and long walks around the grounds. It wasn't so much of a hardship – after two years in Calcutta, he was accustomed to more oppressive climates than the English summertime. Oftentimes Alfie found his steps drawing through the woods and up the hill towards the water tower. He saw no sign of Selena Marbury in the building's grimy windows, and was too fearful of encountering her companion to risk knocking on the door.

It was a shame. A friendly face would have done much to lift Alfie's ebbing spirits. It was getting on for three months since he had a proper night's rest and the side effects were becoming increasingly pronounced. He found himself drifting off in the middle of the day only to jerk awake seconds later, much to the surprise of those around him. More disconcertingly, Alfie had conversations where he thought he was listening, only to walk away without remembering a single word that had been said. It was as though he had been condemned to a shadowy limbo, perpetually half awake and half asleep.

Alfie had reluctantly reached the conclusion that Edmund Grenfell hadn't the faintest idea what he was doing, and that the doctor pretended that Alfie's condition was unusual to try and hide his own failings. Perhaps the drink was eroding his capabilities. For all Grenfell's vaunted reputation, there didn't seem to be a single patient whose health was improving. Sampson still wet the bed, Brooke still burst into tears at the slightest provocation, and attendants continued to find stashes of food Lucy Albright had managed to spirit from her plate.

What was worse, nobody *expected* to get better. The patients seemed resigned to wait for their seventeenth birthday and see then whether they would be allowed to return to their families, or face being transferred to an adult institution. With every passing day Alfie came to view Scarbrook House as a luxurious prison, with the doctors and attendants its unusually respectful warders.

He had sent a carefully worded letter to his father voicing his concerns, but to no avail. Lord Mandeville hadn't replied to any of Alfie's letters since he had arrived at the sanatorium. Even though he knew his father was a busy man – and one for whom business could call abroad at the drop of a hat – the absence of any word hurt Alfie more than he cared to admit. There was little point trying to contact Lady Mandeville. Her spells of lethargy left her completely incapacitated and could last for months. Even if she did not expressly say it, Alfie was certain that his mother loved him. But what if Travers had been right after all, and Alfie was now too great an embarrassment to the Mandeville name to warrant any further contact? Would they ignore him until he was cured?

Determined not to be weighed down by such depressing thoughts, Alfie persevered. A week after Harker's funeral he sought out a writing desk in the library and settled down to compose another letter, taking inspiration from the marble bust of Homer blindly eyeballing him from its pedestal. Alfie wrote neatly and carefully, humming a melody to himself as the pen's nib scratched against the paper. Absorbed in his letter, he was startled when a girl's voice chimed in:

"My lady wind, my lady wind,
"Went round about the house to find
"A chink to get her foot in, her foot in."

Alfie looked up to see Maria's reflection in the window. She was leaning her head against a bookshelf, a faraway look in her eyes as she sang. There was a dark smudge on her cheek, presumably from the bucket of ash by her feet. She looked more beautiful than ever, and Alfie felt a fleeting, guilty pang of desire.

"You know this song too?" he asked. "I've had the

tune in my head for weeks, but I can't seem to remember the words."

Maria didn't look at him.

"I only know those lines," she said softly. "Alice used to sing them to me in the workhouse to help me get to sleep."

"Alice? Was that your sister?"

Maria shook her head. "One of the other girls. She couldn't have been much older than I was, but she cared for me as though I was her own. I wonder what she would do if she could see me now, surrounded by all this finery. Laugh herself silly, I imagine."

Alfie laid down his pen. "Listen, Maria," he began uncomfortably, "about the other day ... what Travers said ... it was uncalled for, and I'm sorry he said it. I blame it on the port. I'm sure that he regrets it."

"Ha!" Maria's eyes came alive with scorn. "That boy regrets nothing. If you've got any sense," she added, "you'll keep a goodly distance between yourself and William Travers, or you'll both end up Below Stairs."

Although Alfie had seen the dark stairwell on his first tour of Scarbrook, it had taken time to learn about "Below Stairs". The patients showed a marked reluctance to talk about it, and the doctors wouldn't even acknowledge its existence. Eventually Alfie had wheedled the truth out of Rothermere; the giant boy fidgeted uncomfortably as he explained. Below Stairs was where the unmanageable patients were taken – the ones considered beyond help, those who screamed continuously and soiled their beds, who bit and scratched the staff, who took too many pills and drank stolen bottles of rat poison to hurt themselves. No one was actually sure what lay beyond the padlocked door at the bottom of the stairwell, but there were hushed reports of padded cells, laboratories and midnight experiments. A popular dare was to run down the stairwell, touch the door and return without getting caught by the staff – or having the crazed inhabitants drag you inside. The secrecy shrouding Below Stairs only enhanced its reputation, turning it into the most terrible of threats:

> *"Finish your vegetables, or you'll be sent Below Stairs,*
> *"Say you're ugly, or you'll be sent Below Stairs,*
> *"Give me a kiss, or you'll be sent Below Stairs,*
> *"Go to bed, or you'll be sent Below Stairs."*

"I know Travers' tongue can be rough, but he isn't all bad," Alfie told Maria. "He's been very kind to me since I arrived here. And I know that you like him too."

"It's not a question of 'liking', Alfie," Maria retorted. "The bonds between myself and William are much darker and more powerful than that, and I bitterly regret the day I ever let him take such a hold of me. And you will too, mark my words."

She picked up the bucket of ashes and walked out of the library, closing the door quietly behind her. Alfie tried to return to his correspondence, but his train of thought had been disturbed and eventually he gave up, folded the letter and went outside to lie in the sun.

*

Three weeks after his arrival at Scarbrook, Alfie lost patience waiting for dawn's arrival and rose before the other boys had awoken. Determined to clear his head – and exhaust himself into a good night's sleep – he skipped breakfast and strode out on his own for a walk.

Tired of his usual route through the woods, Alfie crossed the lawn and passed beneath a stone archway into the sanatorium's rock garden. He found himself in a maze of narrow twisting paths between large moss-covered stones and tangles of ivy and bramble. In a niche between two rocks, a statue of a small, curly-haired boy with a cherubic expression pressed a flute to his lips. Alfie's mood seemed to be lightening, which he put down to the invigorating effect of the sun rising overhead, evaporating the clouds of tiredness hanging over him.

He emerged from the rocky labyrinth through another archway, coming out by the side of Scarbrook's lake. It was a murky green expanse with tangles of wild plant life visible beneath the surface. An iron bridge arched over its middle, its railings glinting in the sunlight. Benches were positioned at regular intervals along the lake's edge, offering passers-by a chance to sit and watch the ducks splashing amongst the reeds.

Alfie was about to take a seat when the sound of female voices pulled him up. Gripped by the sudden fear that his presence might somehow be deemed improper, he ducked behind a tree.

"I think I'll sit here for a while," he heard Selena Marbury declare.

Peeking out from around the trunk, Alfie watched as the young Englishwoman settled slowly down on to a bench. Selena was wearing an ankle-length, pale blue dress, and carried a parasol of the same delicate shade to protect her alabaster skin from the sunlight's gaze. The elder female companion Alfie had seen outside the water tower was twittering nervously around her like a songbird.

"Miss, are you sure it's wise to leave you here?" she asked. "Your father told me that on no account was I to let you out of my sight."

"And were my father here, no doubt he would be tiresomely insistent upon this point," Selena replied tartly. "But my father is in London, with not the slightest intention of visiting me. So he shall be blissfully unaware if you go and fetch my embroidery as I asked."

"But I don't want you getting flustered, miss."

"I honestly swear, Elsie," said Selena, "that I will become even more flustered if you don't stop your continual fussing. I shall be quite all right here for the moment, thank you. Everyone else will be taking breakfast, so I will not be disturbed for at least another hour, and the fresh air will do me the world of good. Being cooped up in that wretched tower all day is going to give me consumption."

Faced with her mistress' insistence, Elsie had little choice but to bustle away. Selena settled against the bench with a contented sigh, leaning her head back and exposing a glimpse of white neck to the sun.

"Psst!" hissed Alfie. "Selena!"

She glanced over in his direction, blinking with surprise. As Alfie stepped out from behind the tree and sketched a deep bow, Selena let out a low, very unladylike whistle. "Little Lord Mandy Vile!" she exclaimed. "What on earth are *you* doing here?"

Alfie grinned. Amongst the esteemed adults who moved in the upper echelons of the British Empire, Selena Marbury was thought to be as brisk and proper as a cup of Assam tea. The select handful of people the Viceroy's daughter drew into her confidence knew better. In fact, Selena was an explosively strong cocktail, laced with mischief and prickly humour. She hid her true nature with the effortless guile of a secret agent, like a blade concealed in a petticoat's folds.

Selena shifted her dress to one side, clearing a space on the bench so that Alfie could sit beside her.

"Believe it or not," he confessed, taking a seat, "I'm also an honoured guest of Dr Grenfell's."

Selena wrinkled her nose. "The man's a weasel," she declared. "He could have been the finest physician in Europe if only he could have kept off the bottle. But instead he's here, and now he cares less about his patients' health than the size of their family's bank accounts. What ailment of yours is he pretending to treat?"

"I can't sleep."

"You do look dreadful," Selena observed critically. "The circles under your eyes look like sunken tar pits."

"Kind of you to say so," Alfie said wryly. He glanced at

Selena, shielding his eyes with his hands. "I've missed you, you know. My father had to return to England so quickly that I never got a chance to say goodbye in Calcutta. And after what happened at the Governor's Ball, I . . . well. . ."

"Don't give it another thought," Selena said firmly. "I don't waste my time lingering upon that particular evening, so neither should you."

A flotilla of ducks bobbed past them on the water, quacking contentedly as they milled about. Alfie cleared his throat nervously.

"I've heard rumours," he confessed. "About what happened in India after I left. About why you're here."

Selena's jaw tightened. "I presumed word would get round sooner rather than later," she said tartly. "People complain about servants gossiping, but the labouring classes have nothing on the nobility when it comes to loose lips and tittle-tattle."

"Is is true? Did you really tear up your clothes and hit a servant girl? And throw a drink at your father?"

"As you said, you'd left," retorted Selena. "You weren't there, so you can't judge me. You never met Lizzie."

Alfie frowned. "Who's that?"

Selena let out a long sigh and looked out over the lake. "She arrived in Calcutta a few weeks after the Governor's Ball," she explained finally. "I was delighted – you'd gone and I felt like I didn't have a friend left in the world. Lizzie and I quickly became close. It was nice to have another girl my own age to share secrets and confidences with. But gradually I began to see a side of Lizzie I didn't like so much: flashes of cruelty and viciousness. She began daring me to do things – only silly things at first. But then it became more serious. I tried to refuse, but she would get so angry it was frightening. So I carried out her dares: tearing up my clothes, embarrassing my father, attacking that poor girl. . ." Selena bit her lip. "I bitterly regret it all, but I was scared that if I didn't do what Lizzie told me, she would hurt me."

"That's horrible!" Alfie exclaimed. "Why didn't you tell your father about her?"

"I tried, but he was too angry with me. He said he didn't want to hear any excuses. Instead he packed me on a boat back to England, where the good doctors of Harley Street were too busy poking and prodding me to actually listen to me. Acute hysteria, indeed! What utter nonsense. You should see the way people look at me now. It's not just embarrassment, or even shame; it's fear. As if I have something infectious that they can catch."

She winced and straightened up, her hand straying to her left arm.

"What is it?" asked Alfie.

"Nothing," Selena replied briskly, bending her arm at the elbow. "My left arm has developed a tendency to lose all feeling from time to time. It's a bit disconcerting. You'd have thought one of the *many* doctors I've seen could have helped me, but apparently it's something else I've dreamt up." She glanced at Alfie. "You believe me, though, don't you? About Lizzie?"

"Of course I do!" he replied loyally.

Selena lapsed into a moody silence, so he tried to change the subject, bringing up happier memories from their time together in Calcutta. But the Viceroy's daughter didn't seem to hear him, her eyes fixed on some distant, unseen point across the lake.

"I should probably go," Alfie said finally. "If someone catches us talking we'll only get into more trouble."

As he rose from the bench, Selena's hand latched on to his. "Don't forget about me, Little Lord Mandy Vile," she said, with sudden urgency. "I have an awful feeling about this place. Something is dreadfully wrong here. Don't leave me all alone. Don't leave me all alone with *her*."

A prickle of unease ran down the back of Alfie's neck. "Who? Lizzie? Are you saying she's here at Scarbrook?"

"I was sure I'd left her behind in Calcutta," Selena said warily. "But sometimes, late at night in that water tower, I'm convinced that someone's there, watching me. You don't think Lizzie could have followed me all the way from India, do you?"

"Of course not," Alfie replied. "Try not to worry, Selena. I'll see you again soon. I promise."

Footsteps along the pathway heralded Elsie's imminent return. Alfie raced off into the trees, Selena's fierce gaze burning a hole in the back of his neck.

CHAPTER SIX

THE PUNKAWALLAH'S SON

By the time Alfie had returned from the lake, the other patients had finished their breakfast and were spilling out into the sunshine. For once the girls had left their drawing room to enjoy the summer morning. Mindful of the watching female attendants, they sat in small circles upon the baked grass a modest distance from the boys. Their presence was enough to make the boys shout a little louder and run a little faster as they messed about and play-fought, each of them secretly hoping to impress. All except one.

Travers stood in the shade of a plum tree, his face a picture of amusement as he watched Rothermere clumsily chasing a rabbit across the grass. He was so still that his every gesture – as discreet as a yawn or a smile, or the tucking of a lock of hair behind his ear – drew the eye. Most of the girls were watching him surreptitiously, and one was openly staring. Lucy Albright always seemed to be close at hand when Travers was around. She was a pretty girl with long blonde hair, but her face was gaunt and the wrists poking out from the sleeves of her dress were painfully thin. When her friend Constance, a talkative girl with dark frizzy hair, gave her a nudge and whispered something in her ear, Lucy blushed and looked away from the plum tree.

From a distance, the scene could have been mistaken for a cheery Sunday afternoon in Greenwich or Clapham. It was the little details that suggested there was something slightly amiss – the girl sitting on her own, sobbing and pulling at her hair; the barrel-armed male attendants, standing watchful guard over the boys; and in the background, Scarbrook's bruised brickwork looming over the patients like a warning.

As Alfie approached, a boy broke away from the melee to speak to him. It was Sampson, the thin, bespectacled boy who couldn't stop wetting the bed. He looked down at the ground as he spoke. "Dr Grenfell wants to see you, Alfie."

"Oh, right. Thanks."

Alfie trudged off the sunlit lawn and entered Scarbrook, the shrieks of laughter dying away as the building swallowed him up. Time seemed to move more slowly in the muggy, second-hand air; dust particles drifted lazily through beams of light. Further along the corridor Alfie caught a glimpse of Yardley and Catherine creeping inside the library. The two siblings seemed to exist in their own little world, completely out of step with the other patients.

Inside Edmund Grenfell's study the blinds had been drawn over the windows, keeping the room dark and cool. The doctor rose from behind his desk as Alfie entered and invited him to lie down upon the divan.

"I have been giving your situation some consideration, Master Mandeville," he said, pulling up a chair beside him, "and I believe it may be time to try something radical. Have you heard of hypnotism?"

"Yes, sir."

"Good, good. It is a controversial field," Grenfell admitted, fishing a watch out from his pocket, "and some of my colleagues claim that its practitioners are little better than fraudsters or cardsharps, but I prefer to keep an open mind. With such a stubborn and unusual case as yours, I wonder whether a more unorthodox treatment could induce a more encouraging response. So, if you're feeling comfortable, let us begin. If you could just maintain your gaze upon my timepiece..."

The doctor swung his watch back and forth in front of Alfie's eyes, the metal surface catching a stray beam of sunlight slicing through the blinds. As he followed its glinting arc, Alfie felt his shoulders slowly relax and his mind begin to drift. He allowed himself to follow Grenfell's soft suggestions, mentally walking out of the study and descending down a long staircase. It wasn't the deep enveloping of sleep – more a pleasant daydream, which led him out of the darkness and blinking into the light...

Take me back to the beginning, Alfie. The beginning of this whole story. Where are you?

Dr Grenfell's voice echoed commandingly inside Alfie's head.

"Our house," he replied.

In Chelsea?

"No. Calcutta."

Alfie was stretched out upon the bed in a room with whitewashed walls. Even though the day's light was fading, the room was as hot as an oven, and Alfie's skin was coated in sweat. The insistent chirp of crickets carried in through the open window.

What are you doing?

"Nothing. I . . . I was sleeping."

Alfie's head was throbbing and his mouth was parched. He rose from his bed and walked over to the window, disturbing a small lizard clinging to the wall. It scurried away behind the bureau, its green skin brilliant with indignation at being disturbed. The familiar outline of Calcutta's skyline was visible through the encroaching gloom: nearby, the grand white columns and domes of the neighbouring mansions and imperial offices; further north, the haphazard terraces and parapets of the Indian dwellings. In the distance, ships' masts poked out like matchsticks above the buildings on the banks of the Hooghly River. With the day's trading done, and many of its British inhabitants taking their late afternoon naps, the city was cloaked in a deep hush.

Quiet also reigned within the Mandeville house. Earlier that afternoon, before Alfie had fallen asleep, there had been raised voices downstairs. Upon the front door slamming, Alfie had raced over to the window in time to see his father striding angrily away from the house. If their previous arguments were anything to go by, Lord Mandeville would still be in the Bombay Club, lost in a fug of cigar smoke, whilst Lady Mandeville would have retired to her bedroom with her bottle of laudanum. Alfie's mother had been prescribed the drug to help with her lethargic "shades", but judging by her increasing absent-mindedness and dreamlike demeanour, the laudanum was doing more harm than good.

Leaving his room, Alfie crept through the empty hallways of his house like a sneak thief. Previously warm and familiar objects took on an ominous presence amid the lengthening shadows. Busts glared at Alfie, smiling faces in paintings turned to scowls. Where was Stowbridge? The Indian servants might have gone home for the day, but the Mandeville's butler had his own quarters in the house. He was never far away.

As Alfie carefully descended the main staircase, he stopped abruptly on the bottom step.

What is it?

"There are people downstairs," whispered Alfie.

The door to the drawing room was ajar, allowing a faint murmur of voices to escape out into the hallway. Alfie crept up to the door and peered through the crack.

The shutters had been fastened over the dining room windows, leaving a handful of tall candles to battle against the darkness. In the flickering orange light Alfie saw a group of people sitting around a table in the centre of the room, their clasped hands forming a trembling ring. There were two men and two women – Stowbridge and the Viceroy, a lady Alfie didn't recognize, and Lady Mandeville. The strange woman's eyes were tightly closed, and she was chanting something under her breath. Everyone was watching her, waiting. The atmosphere was thick with cloying incense and tension.

The woman suddenly stopped chanting, and the candles flinched as one. Lady Mandeville moaned with fear, and even Stowbridge's jawline tightened. The Viceroy alone seemed pleased, leaning forward and asking eagerly:

"Can you hear them, Amelia?"

The woman nodded.

"What are they saying to you?"

"Many things ... difficult to understand ... too many voices. . ."

"What about Victoria?" urged the Viceroy. "Is my Victoria there?"

"I don't know ... so many voices. . ."

"Find her for me! Find my Victoria!"

"I feel something ... a presence ... could it be?"

A loud rapping sound made Alfie start. It was as though someone had knocked upon the table, but that was impossible, because everyone gathered was still holding hands.

"She is here!" Amelia wailed.

"Can it be?" the Viceroy cried. "Victoria?"

He stumbled to his feet, a look of blissful joy upon his face. Alfie felt suddenly uncomfortable, aware that he was spying on something private. He edged away from the door, retreating into the shadows of the corridor.

"Poppycock!" a voice whispered in his ear.

He almost bit his tongue in fright. Whirling around, Alfie was confronted by a girl his own age in a lace dress, a knowing smile upon her face.

"Selena!" hissed Alfie. "You scared the life out of me! What do you think you're doing?"

Selena Marbury, daughter of Edward Marbury, Viceroy of India, replied by sticking out her tongue. Her skin may have been pale and her features as delicate as a porcelain doll's, but mischief danced in her eyes and her lips were armed with a ready retort. She beckoned Alfie away from the drawing room and moved smartly through the house towards the back verandah. Alfie followed her, as he always did.

Their friendship had initially been one of convenience. Most of their friends of the same age had been sent back to Britain to continue their education at boarding school. Lord Mandeville had surprised Alfie by declaring that he was to remain in Calcutta, asserting that there was greater merit to be found seeing the family business at first hand than conjugating Latin verbs. Selena had also stayed in India, her widowed father unable to contemplate separation from his beloved daughter. Aware that their children couldn't spend all their time in polite company – and that mixing with the locals was out of the question – the Viceroy and the Mandevilles allowed Alfie and Selena to spend the occasional afternoon together. Alfie quickly warmed to Selena, marvelling at her unpredictability and sense of fun, whilst she seemed to take equal pleasure in teasing him. They were now best friends – not that either of them would have admitted it.

A slight breeze was creeping on to the verandah, rustling the leaves of the climbing plants and easing the stifling heat. Selena plumped herself down upon the swing and groaned loudly.

"This evening has been the most crashing bore!" she complained. "Where on earth have you been?"

"Asleep in my room. Sorry. Nobody told me you were coming."

"It was a last-minute arrangement. My father only told me our destination when we had picked up that ghastly Amelia Brockhurst woman."

Who would have to have been the strange woman leading the séance. "Why is she ghastly?" asked Alfie.

Selena's face darkened. "She's a stupid troublemaker who claims to be a medium and fills my father's head with all sorts of nonsense about spirits and the other side."

"You think it's nonsense?"

"Oh, *please* don't tell me you believe all that mumbo jumbo." Selena waggled her fingers, impersonating a witch casting a spell.

"I don't know," Alfie said carefully, "but I'm not sure you should mock things you don't understand. Your father believes in spirits, doesn't he?"

Selena sighed. "My father – whom I love very, very

dearly – is a lonely fool who thinks that by lighting a few candles he can somehow speak to my mother."

"And you think he's wrong?"

"My mother's dead, Alfie," Selena said abruptly. "There's nothing more to say about it."

She looked out over the Mandevilles' back garden, which had become a tangle of silhouettes as the evening deepened into night. As the breeze dropped, Selena's gaze fell upon a large fern beneath the verandah. It was still rustling. Her eyes narrowed.

"There's something out there," she told Alfie quietly.

Alfie jumped to his feet. Two years in Calcutta had taught him that the Indian undergrowth could hide greater threats than the badgers or foxes at home. There were tales of stinging ants attacking picnics, and vicious scorpions nesting in piles of laundry. Only two months previous, a servant had stumbled across a cobra coiled beneath Lady Mandeville's chest of drawers. It was a miracle nobody had been bitten.

Whilst Alfie scrabbled about for a stick, Selena leaned over the verandah rail and addressed the fern in an imperious tone.

"I say, who's there? Come on out now!"

A dark-skinned boy with tousled hair stepped out of the bushes. Alfie recognized him instantly. It was Ajay, the punkawallah's son. Punkawallahs were servants who worked the giant slatted fans on the ceiling, continually pulling at them with lengths of rope. Whilst his father kept the fans moving, Ajay earned coins running messages for the Mandeville household. Though he always tried to be friendly and polite to the servants, Alfie had never taken to Ajay. There was something in the boy's silent gaze he found unsettling.

"What are you doing there?" Alfie asked crossly. "Were you spying on us?"

Ajay ignored Alfie, his gaze completely fixed upon Selena. He appeared to be in some kind of trance. The Viceroy's daughter didn't appear bothered in the slightest. In fact, there was the slightest hint of a smile playing on her lips. Irritated, Alfie picked up a stone and hurled it at Ajay.

"Go on – get out of here!" he shouted. "Before I tell my father!"

The spell broken, Ajay turned and ran away down the garden, quickly melting into the darkness.

"Stupid boy," muttered Alfie.

"Aren't you all?" Selena replied archly.

"I should tell my father."

"Oh, leave it, Alfie. He's harmless." Selena laid a hand upon Alfie's arm. "Thank you for saving me, though. You are my knight in shining armour. Let's give you a suitably grand title. Hmm ... nothing too common, only a lord will do here – Lord Alfred. No, that's too formal... Lord Mande ... Lord Mandy Vile." Selena's eyes brightened. "Perfect."

A loud crash and a cry from within the house cut off her laughter. Alfie raced inside, bumping into the Viceroy in the corridor. Selena's father had stormed from the drawing room and was making for the front door, a shell-shocked Amelia Brockhurst in tow.

"This is an outrage, Mandeville!" he shouted, shaking a fist. "This isn't the last you'll hear about this, mark my words!"

Spying his daughter behind Alfie, the Viceroy grabbed her by the wrist and marched her out through the front door, ignoring Selena's protests. Alfie had already forgotten about them, his eyes fixed on the scene inside the drawing room. The furniture was in a state of disarray, the table on its side and chairs scattered about. One of the candles had been knocked to the floor, and Stowbridge was frantically stamping out the flames on the carpet. Lady Mandeville had collapsed in a heap on the floor in a flurry of skirts, sobbing bitterly. Above her stood a vision of rage.

Alfie struggled to describe what he saw. The man was his father, and yet not. Lord Mandeville was neat and meticulous, handsome and upright. This man's eyes were wild, and his whole body trembled with fury. His collar was open, his clothes dishevelled, and he reeked of spirits. His appearance had even caused Stowbridge – usually an implacable mask – to look uncertain. For Alfie, who had never seen his father with so much as a hair out of place, it was a truly horrifying sight.

"Didn't I tell you not to meddle with these things?" Lord Mandeville roared.

"Forgive me, Robert!" cried Alfie's mother, shying away. "I know I promised."

"You lied! That's all you do – you lie and you meddle and you lie and you meddle! Damned woman!"

As he raised his arm as though to strike her, Stowbridge stepped forward and placed a restraining hand on his master's elbow. Lord Mandeville spun round, astonished that his servant had dared to touch him. It was then that he caught sight of Alfie huddling in the doorway.

"And what do you think you're looking at?" Lord Mandeville snarled. "Get out of here, you little devil!"

Alfie fled from the drawing room, haring up the stairs and back into the safety of his bedroom, where he slammed the door behind him and leaned against it. His chest felt so tight he could hardly breathe.

Alfie? Are you all right?

Dr Grenfell's voice again, from somewhere very far away.

I'm going to clap my hands…

Alfie sat up on Dr Grenfell's divan, his heart pounding in his chest. India had vanished – the crickets silenced, the candles extinguished – and he was back in the gentle heat of the English summer.

"Breathe, Alfred," he heard the doctor say. "You'll be fine in a minute. Just take deep, slow breaths."

"That was so real!" Alfie gasped. "Just like I was back in the room! What *was* that?"

"A good start," said Dr Grenfell, patting him on the arm. "A very good start indeed."

CHAPTER SEVEN

SHADOW PUPPETS

Alfie walked out of the study in a daze. Dr Grenfell had seemed genuinely excited by the results of the hypnotism, praising Alfie's powers of recollection. When he casually asked Alfie whether he had seen Selena since his return from India, Alfie was careful to lie and say no. After all, if the doctor found out that people knew she was staying in the water tower, Selena might get into trouble.

Alfie wasn't sure what he made of it all. He had pushed the unhappy memory of his mother's séance down into a deep burrow in his mind, and he felt no better for having it dug up again. What was the point? It had taken place over six months before his insomnia had started – what possible link could there be? If this was progress, Dr Grenfell was getting desperate.

His mind shadowed with doubt, Alfie drifted aimlessly through the hallways and corridors of Scarbrook House, unwilling to rejoin the others outside on the lawn. He headed away from the sunlit rooms and deeper into the bowels of the building, down a staircase that led towards the kitchens. Patients were supposedly forbidden from coming this way, but then Scarbrook was such a labyrinth there was no practical way of stopping them. Anyway, there was little in the way of riches to be found down here, unless pantries and sculleries counted as treasure vaults, and sacks of grain and laundry priceless plunder.

Alfie's mind was elsewhere as he stepped down into the gloomy corridor at the bottom of the staircase, and he nearly slipped on a wet flagstone. Peering down at his feet, he was surprised to see a shallow tide of water ebbing across the floor. Intrigued, Alfie splashed further into the darkness in search of the source of the flood. He found it at the end of the corridor, where water was gushing out from beneath a scullery door. When Alfie pressed his ear against the door, he heard a girl's muffled voice yell:

"I'll kill you!"

Alfie tried the handle, but the door was locked. He took a short run-up and charged it with his shoulder, splinters exploding into the air as the door gave way. Alfie stumbled into the scullery to find it ankle-deep in water. The taps were flooding into an overflowing sink and down on to the floor, where metal pans and laundry whites floated upon the tide. In the middle of the scullery Maria and Travers were facing off against each other on either side of a table. Maria's cheeks were inflamed with colour and there was a murderous look in her eyes. Travers was grinning with spiteful glee, circling the table as the serving girl hissed and clawed at him.

"Stop it!" Alfie cried. "What's going on?"

"Stay out of it!" snarled Travers.

Maria didn't even appear to have heard Alfie. She glanced over towards the work surface, where a knife lay gleaming on the chopping board.

Travers chuckled darkly. "Don't you get any crazy ideas, you thieving little hellcat. Someone might get hurt."

Maria screeched with fury and spat in his face. Travers growled and lunged across the table at her, but she leapt out of the way and ran for the scullery door, foreign curses echoing down the corridor as she fled.

When the shouts and footfalls had faded, the scullery fell quiet. All Alfie could hear was the gushing of the taps and Travers' halting breaths. The elder boy had turned very slowly to face Alfie, and was staring at him with bestial hatred.

"Now look here, Travers," Alfie began. "That was—"

Travers grabbed him roughly, pinning his arms to his sides.

"Who asked you to get involved, you little rodent?" he hissed. "Do you want Maria for yourself? Is that it? Has the wench wrapped you around her little finger?" Travers pressed his face up close against Alfie's. "Or is it me you'd prefer, you deviant? Is that what keeps you up all night – being so close to all those boys? Is that why big, brave Lord Mandeville is so ashamed he won't even reply to your letters?"

Alfie shoved Travers away, tears springing to his eyes. "You're ill in the head," he said fiercely.

There was a pause and then, to Alfie's astonishment, Travers burst out laughing. "Well, of course I am!" he exclaimed, with startling frivolity. "Why else would I be here?"

As Alfie dried his eyes upon his sleeve, the other boy scratched his head, looking around the ruined scullery as if for the first time. "What a mess!" he exclaimed, looking down at his sodden legs. "I wouldn't be surprised if the water has ruined a perfectly good pair of trousers."

"Is that really all you care about?" Alfie said incredulously.

Travers let out a long, heartfelt sigh. "My dear Alfie," he said quietly, "please forgive my horrible outburst. It was terribly poor form. When Maria and I fight like that I quite lose control. Could you see your way to accepting my apology and us becoming friends again?"

Alfie looked mistrustfully at Travers' extended hand.

"My good-hearted, innocent Mandeville," the boy continued, "you must understand that not all relationships can run as smoothly as you might wish. Maria and I are a complicated affair, no doubt, but for every wrong I do her she repays me in kind. Not every member of the fairer sex need be a victim, Alfie."

Alfie hesitated. "I don't know what to think," he admitted.

"Allow me to try and make it up to you. Seeing as we're down here, let's go to the kitchens and see if we can charm the cook into giving us some fresh pastries."

"I should really go and check on Maria," Alfie said doubtfully. "I'd like to make sure that she's all right."

"Make sure that *she's* all right?" A look of mock-offence crossed Travers' face. "If you must play Florence Nightingale, it should be your poor friend W. Travers to whom you attend. Maria will be fine, mark my words. I was the one spat in the face – I am the one at risk of contracting typhus, or some other savage disease."

Alfie shook his head. "It's not always easy being your friend, William, do you know that? There are times when I think you are cruel for the sake of it."

"I know," he replied. "There are times when I think that too. Come on, Lord Mandeville. Let's get you out of here."

Alfie allowed Travers to steer him out of the room through the jagged remnants of the doorway, leaving the taps to continue their gushing lament behind them.

That evening Alfie sat alone in his bed, his knees pulled up to his chest as he wrote. The candle at his bedside spluttered as it divided the empty dormitory into two colours: a warm, illuminating orange, and the long black shadows of bed railings and wardrobes that slanted across the walls like giant fingers. Alfie's pen nib made a satisfying scratch as he guided it across the paper, an old encyclopedia resting against his knees as a stand-in desk.

The doctor says we are making progress, Father, and that my sleeping pattern is improving rapidly, wrote Alfie, the lie flowing easily from his pen. *I hope that very soon I shall*

be able to return to London and see you and Mother. Perhaps
you could make arrangements for a carriage to pick me up next
week? It was a desperate, deceitful ploy, Alfie knew, but
he didn't care. He didn't even care if Lord Mandeville
found out that he was lying. Let him check! His father
could write to him calling him an embarrassment and an
unworthy son if he wanted; at least it would be contact.
Nothing could hurt as much as the deafening silence that
greeted Alfie's correspondence, this sense that his parents
weren't even aware of his existence any more. That he
was as dead to them as Harker was to his parents.

Alfie put down his pen and rubbed his eyes with ink-
smudged fingers. His eyes were always hot and itchy these
days, as though the lack of sleep had given him hay fever.
This day had drained him more than usual. Even though
Travers had apologized for what had happened between
them, Alfie found it hard to shake the images from the
scullery from his mind, and dinner found him with
little appetite. Tired of pushing food around his plate, he
headed up to the dormitory early, ignoring the mocking
chorus of "Sleep well" and "Sweet dreams" that greeted
his exit. In a funny way, the fact that the others felt able
to tease him about his condition was a sign that he had
been accepted. Alfie was truly one of Scarbrook's patients
now, whether he wanted to be or not.

In the distance, a small bell rang. It sounded as
though Dr Grenfell had decided upon a new way to
signal the patients' bedtime. Alfie tapped his pen on the
paper, trying to think of a neat way to end his letter.

I hope that Mother has recovered fully from her latest illness, and that she is sufficiently recovered that you can pass on her son's l —

The pen nib stopped in its tracks. Alfie could have sworn he saw something move on the other side of the room, over by Yardley's bed. He put down his pen and peered cautiously over his knees. Rothermere had warned him to keep an eye out for Perkins, who loved playing practical jokes to scare the other patients, but there was no sign of the redhead by Yardley's bed – or anybody else, for that matter. Alfie picked up his pen again.

— ove. Your faithful son, Alf

Invisible freckles of fear broke out over Alfie's skin. He had definitely seen something this time, out of the corner of his eye. But what? He pretended to return to his letter, all the while keeping his gaze trained on the other side of the room.

There. A dark shape darting between two beds, the outline of a boy. A shadow. But no boy.

Alfie rubbed his eyes in disbelief.

The shadow rolled out from the other side of the bed and sprang up to the top of a nearby wardrobe, making its way from shadow to shadow like a frog hopping across pond lilies. It clambered up on to a shelf and swung across the dormitory door, landing neatly on the silhouette of a bedside table on Alfie's side of the room. Alfie watched, open-mouthed. It was like an image cast from a magic lantern, the enactment of some dark fairy tale. An impossible dance.

The shadow bounded up on top of Alfie's wardrobe and sank into a crouch, looking down upon him. Its face was a blank, featureless mask. As it waited, motionless, Alfie heard a bell ringing once more, and felt a stirring of alarm deep in the pit of his stomach. Too late. The shadow sprang down from the wardrobe on top of him, its hands outstretched.

Alfie tried to shout for help, but as his mouth opened the shadow was upon him, pinning him to the bed. He felt the dark's essence seeping inside him, filling his mouth. There was no smell or taste, and all he could see was black. A crushing pressure was pushing down on him and filling his lungs. It felt as though he was drowning. Alfie thrashed about on the bed in complete silence, mummified in shadow. He wanted to be sick but his throat was too full. As he writhed, he caught sight of the candle on his table. The only source of light in the room. The only source of shadow.

In a final act of desperation, Alfie forced his head off the pillow and blew out the candle. At once the room tumbled into darkness, the shadows melting away to nothing, including the one that had smothered him. All Alfie was left with was the aftertaste of terror in his mouth, and the sound of his own hoarse, petrified breaths.

When the other boys came up to the room ten minutes later, they found Alfie curled up in a ball on the floor by his bed. He was shivering uncontrollably, his bedclothes drenched with sweat.

"Good Lord, Alfie," Travers exclaimed. "Whatever's happened?"

"S-s-shadow," Alfie managed to reply, through chattering teeth. "Tried to h-h-hurt me."

They lifted him up and put him back to bed, murmuring reassurances. It was a while before Alfie could tell them what had happened. They listened in silence as he explained, haltingly at first, and then the words came spilling out and he had to stop himself from bursting into tears. If Alfie had thought that the boys would laugh at his story, he was in for a surprise. They glanced at one another, their faces grave.

"I'm sorry you've had such a fright, Alfie," said Travers. "But I'm sure there's a rational explanation for it."

"Shadows don't just attack people," added Perkins. "Not even here."

"I know it sounds strange," said Alfie, "but it really did happen. If only you'd come up when the bell rang, maybe you would have seen it too."

Travers frowned. "What bell?"

"It rang just before. . ."

Alfie trailed off in the face of the other boys' incomprehension. Whatever he had heard, they hadn't.

"The graveyard," a voice said quietly. The boys turned as one to look at Yardley.

"Meaning what precisely, Yardley?" asked Perkins.

"We heard a bell ring in the graveyard too. When they buried Harker."

"I think we can rule Harker out as a suspect," the redhead said dryly. "What with him being dead and all."

"Can you really be so sure? Who had Alfie's bed before him?"

The answer hung heavily in the air, and there was a long silence as the boys stared at one another. Then Travers groaned loudly. "Is everyone going stark raving mad? You can't be listening to this claptrap! Alfie had a nightmare, plain and simple!"

"And why would Harker attack Alfie anyway?" piped up Brooke. "They'd never even met! It doesn't make any sense!"

"Who said he was trying to attack him?" asked Yardley. "Maybe Harker was just trying to return to a safe place."

"I suppose the spirit world told you that, didn't it?" said Travers, with withering scorn.

Alfie wasn't listening to Travers any more. He was watching Yardley intently. The smaller boy held his gaze without blinking, serene as an angel.

"But if he wasn't trying to attack me, then what did he want, Yardley?" Alfie whispered. "What was Harker trying to say?"

"Help me," replied Yardley.

CHAPTER EIGHT

I SEE YOU

That night Alfie welcomed the darkness as his friend – in a world of black, there could be no shadows. Yet as the hours ticked by, he became more and more convinced that his vision had been the result of a bad dream. Shadows couldn't leap off the walls and attack people. That was insane! In the next bed, Travers turned over in his sleep, nodding his head and muttering unintelligibly as though in agreement.

Morning revealed an army of frowning clouds marching in upon Scarbook House. The air was restless with the threat of storms. A loud clap of thunder during breakfast made everyone jump, and sent Brooke running from the dining hall for cover. The storm broke mid-morning, hurling raindrops the size of pebbles against the windows. Alfie watched the deluge from an armchair in the drawing room, his thoughts drifting back to Calcutta. During the monsoon season the narrow streets of the Indian quarter would become flooded, forcing the locals to take off their shoes and carry them above their heads as they waded through the muddy water.

The crackling atmosphere was unsettling some of the more fragile patients. Two of the girls had to be separated by a female attendant during an argument over a pincushion, whilst Sampson marched up and down the drawing room like a guard on a midnight watch, his hands behind his back and his head bowed. As Alfie watched him pace back and forth, Travers appeared in the doorway, moving with the furtiveness of a secret agent. He pushed an armchair next to Alfie's and took a seat.

"Listen, I've been thinking about last night," Travers said quietly, "and maybe I was wrong to doubt you. At the time your story sounded too fantastical to be true, but then this is Scarbrook. Strange things happen here, there's no denying it. You told me you were attacked, and I should have taken your word as a gentleman."

"No, Travers, you were right," Alfie replied. "The more I think about it, the more I realize it must have been a nightmare. It's the only rational explanation."

"Do you want to make sure?" Travers waited until Sampson had paced out of earshot before continuing in a whisper, "Do you want to find out if Harker really did have anything to do with it?"

"How?"

He grinned. "How do you think? We'll ask him."

"I hate to point this out, Travers, but Harker's dead," said Alfie. "What are you going to do — send him a telegram?"

The elder boy put a finger to his lips. "Meet me after lunch," he said, rising from his chair and slipping out of the room.

As the storm's ferocity increased, an early dusk fell over the sanatorium, and the patients ate their lunch by candlelight. Despite the thundering rain it was still suffocatingly warm inside Scarbrook, and as Alfie followed Travers out of the dining hall he could feel the sweat gather in his armpits and on the small of his back. They went quickly and quietly through the corridors, Travers glancing around to check that no one was following them. In the Main Hall they paused beneath the painting of Sir Thomas Scarbrook and waited for an attendant to climb the stairs before hurrying through the doorway into the east wing.

The fire-ravaged rooms were off-limits to the patients, and Alfie went watchfully from one scene of devastation to another. The smell of burned wood, to which he had become so accustomed that he now barely noticed it, returned with a vengeance. Each room had been reduced to the same piteous state – blackened walls, charred remnants of tables and chairs, and other objects that were little more than scorched shells and husks, with only the vaguest hints to their former shape and purpose. No longer rooms, but eye sockets.

The final room was a dirty, bleak hole. Rain fell like tears through a hole in the ceiling: Alfie could see the grey maelstrom in the skies overhead. A small knot of patients had gathered in the room to wait for them. There was Silas Rothermere, sitting awkwardly cross-legged on the floor, and Lucy and her friend Constance Cherwell. At the sight of Travers, Lucy's eyes lit up.

"Look at this place," said Alfie, with a shake of the head.

"I heard this was where the fire started," said Travers.

"I can't believe Yardley did this."

"Didn't you hear?" Travers said innocently. "He didn't do it. It was the spirit world's fault."

His laughter echoed around the charred room. Reaching down behind the remains of a bureau, Travers pulled out a flat object wrapped in a sheet. He whipped off the sheet with a flourish, revealing a battered playing board.

"What've you got there, then?" said Rothermere curiously.

It was Alfie who answered. "It's a oujia board," he said. Whilst exploring the attic of their house in Chelsea, Alfie had stumbled across a dusty wooden box with his mother's initials on the lid. Inside he had found several books on spiritualism and a photograph of two young men smiling at the camera: Lord Mandeville, and a handsome blond man Alfie guessed was Frederick Scarbrook. The oujia board was lying at the bottom of the box, complete with a set of instructions. Alfie had been so engrossed reading he hadn't heard Stowbridge on the attic steps: upon seeing him with the board, the butler had hauled Alfie in front of an angry Lord Mandeville to explain himself. Alfie was denied supper for three nights as punishment – the box had been burnt in the back garden that afternoon, together with all its contents.

Travers' board was older and more careworn than

Lady Mandeville's. The letters of the alphabet – listed in two curving rows, one on top of the other – were faded, and the wood was scarred and pockmarked. Beneath the letters there was a row of numbers, from 0 to 9; above them were the words "yes" and "no". Near the right-hand edge of the board was the single word "goodbye".

"What's a *wee-jar* board?" asked Rothermere, his face scrunched up with confusion.

"A communication device," Travers replied. "It can help us talk to the spirits. We can use it to ask Harker if he was the thing that attacked Alfie last night."

"Are you sure about this?" Alfie said doubtfully. "If it was just a bad dream. . ."

". . . then Harker will tell us," replied Travers. "Don't get cold feet now. You're a Mandeville, remember?"

He placed the board down on the floor and told everyone to kneel down around it. Travers produced a heart-shaped wooden pointer from his pocket – a planchette, he called it – and instructed everyone to place their hand upon it. They would act as a channel for the spirit force, spelling out answers to the questions they asked. Alfie did as he was told, sandwiching his hand between Rothermere's sweaty palm and Lucy Albright's cool fingers. The five of them were hunched so close over the board that he could feel the girl's breath upon his cheek. Despite himself, Alfie felt a small thrill of excitement.

"Everybody ready?" asked Travers. Then, in a loud voice: "Who's there?"

For a second, nothing. Then the planchette began to move beneath Alfie's fingers, heading slowly but purposefully across the board. A shiver of excitement ran down his back like a raindrop. The planchette came to rest by the letter H, and then started towards the left-hand side of the board.

"Someone's pushing it," giggled Constance.

"Not me," said Travers.

"Don't look at me!" added Lucy.

Alfie knew he wasn't moving the pointer, and judging by the look of wonder on Rothermere's face, neither was he. It felt as though the planchette was leading them, not the other way around. The patients watched in rapt silence as the pointer continued its journey around the board, spelling a name: H-A-R-K-E-R.

"It's working, Travers!" whispered Rothermere.

"So it would seem," Travers agreed, his face tight with the strain of concentration. "Now let's see if we can find out what it's playing at." In the same commanding tones as before, he said, "Where are you, spirit?"

The planchette rocketed across the board without warning, taking them all by surprise. It hurried to the letter B, before switching to the letter E so abruptly that Rothermere nearly toppled on to the board. With a sense of growing dread, Alfie watched as the spirit spoke to them; next an H and an I and an N and a D and a Y. . .

"Alfie, behind you!" shouted Travers.

Whirling around, Alfie saw a wraithlike figure in

a dark cloak rise up from behind a pile of burned timber. Lucy screamed and ducked behind Rothermere, who covered his face with his hands. The colour drained from Constance's face, and Travers seemed frozen to the spot. As Alfie looked on with horror, the wraith raised a cloaked arm and extended a finger towards him.

As the patients scrambled backwards, the figure's shoulders began to shake, and reedy laughter emerged from the depths of its hood. It reached up and pulled back its cowl, revealing a familiar face with red hair.

"Got you," said Perkins.

In the stunned aftermath, Travers and Perkins collapsed into helpless laughter, slapping each other on the back and pointing at the other patients.

"Look at your faces! Like goldfish!" Travers made an impersonation of a gaping fish, causing Perkins to weep with laughter.

"Travers, you monster!" Constance shouted, as she comforted the wailing Lucy. Rothermere looked utterly bewildered, as though trying to work out whether or not he should still be frightened. Alfie stared at his friend.

"This was all just a silly prank?"

"Call it a valuable lesson," replied Travers. "If you believe Yardley's hokum, you deserve everything you get."

"And what about the others?" Alfie shot back, pointing at Lucy. "Did they deserve it too, then? Or are you just too mean and too selfish to care?"

A pointed silence descended upon the charred room as Alfie and Travers faced off against each other. Travers looked furious at having been challenged, but for once Alfie was too angry to care. He bunched up his fists, ready to start swinging if the other boy came for him.

A low scraping sound made them turn back to the board. Alfie looked down to see that the planchette had moved away from its previous position, and was now pointing at the letter P.

"Who did that?" Constance asked quickly.

"No one," replied Rothermere.

"This isn't funny, Travers."

Travers wasn't laughing.

The planchette twitched, like an animal's nose sniffing the air, before scuttling across to the letter E.

"William, stop it!" cried Lucy.

"It's not me!" he replied, in a voice shot through with shock and fear. "What's going on?"

Every turn of the planchette, every sudden spurt of movement was greeted by fresh wails and moans. Alfie watched, transfixed, as the letters continued. E. . . K. . .

There was a clatter and footsteps as Perkins bolted from the room. No one else dared move.

A. . .

"What it's saying, Alfie?" asked Rothermere.

"I'm not sure yet."

B. . . O. . .

And then he knew exactly what the ouija board was telling them.

The planchette scraped over to the letter O, and then slid over to the word "goodbye". Then it stopped moving.

"Peek-a-boo?" said Rothermere, his face creased with bewilderment. "What does that mean?"

"I see you," Alfie said softly.

Without warning, Constance collapsed as though she had been struck by something. She began to writhe upon the floor, her body racked with spasms.

"She's been possessed!" cried Rothermere.

"Don't be so silly," Lucy replied. "She's having a fit. We need to fetch a doctor."

"No." Travers' voice was firm. "We'll help her. Find something she can bite down on. Nothing metal or she'll break her teeth."

He knelt down beside Constance whilst the others spread out, hunting for a suitable bit. It was Rothermere who found a charred clothes peg and passed it to Travers, who wedged it between Constance's teeth. He whispered soothingly in the girl's ear as she juddered and shook.

Alfie watched on helplessly until the fit began to ease and Constance groggily came round. Though everyone asked her how she was feeling, she seemed less concerned about her health than the possibility of anyone hearing about it.

"Please don't tell anyone," begged Constance. "Please, not a soul!"

"Don't worry!" said Alfie. "We won't."

"My parents think I haven't had a fit for six months," she explained. "You don't know what they'll say if they hear about this. They think I'm mad!"

"Don't let anyone tell you that. You hear me? No one."

It was Travers speaking, but there was something different about his tone. All traces of his habitual mockery had vanished, and his dark brown eyes were deadly earnest.

"There's nothing wrong with you," he said. "You shouldn't even be in Scarbrook in the first place. Don't let your parents and these doctors turn you into something you're not. Don't let *them* make you ill."

He gently lifted up Constance's head and stared at her until eventually she nodded. As he watched his friend escort Constance out of the parlour, Alfie felt his anger and fear ebb away, to be replaced by an unexpected new emotion: grudging admiration.

They stumbled back into the Main Hall, relieved to close the door upon the east wing and its scarred rooms. Travers, Alfie noted, had left the ouija board on the floor of the parlour – the closest he had seen to his friend acknowledging a mistake. Lucy and Constance went up the staircase towards the girls' bedroom without a word, whilst Travers and Rothermere headed for the drawing room. After the unsettling events in the parlour, Alfie felt the need to be alone, and he decided to go to the library to find a new book to read.

He entered the room to find Yardley standing by the fireplace. It looked as though the younger boy had been waiting for him. Catherine was sitting at a desk by the window, engrossed in some wordless game with her doll.

"I heard what you did," said Yardley, without preamble.

"Leave me alone," Alfie said wearily. "I'm too tired for your nonsense."

"You contacted the spirit world. They told me what happened." Yardley spoke in a matter-of-fact tone, as though he were discussing a butler or a maid.

"There's no such thing as the spirit world!" Alfie shouted. "You're just a crazy boy who goes around setting fire to things!"

Catherine got up from the desk and pushed past her brother, her eyes wide with indignation as she stared at Alfie.

"I'm not mad," Yardley said calmly. "I know that there are spirits that move beyond this world. I talk to the good ones, and I hide from the bad ones. But you . . . this afternoon you sat in the ashes and you tried to play a game with evil. It wasn't playing, Alfie. It's been waiting for this moment and now it's on its way."

"Shut up!" cried Alfie. "Stay away from me!"

"Don't you understand?" Yardley insisted, clutching at Alfie's sleeve. "They'll be coming! We're all in danger now!"

Alfie shook off his hand and strode out of the library. Yardley watched him stalk off. "We're all in danger now," he repeated forlornly.

CHAPTER NINE

THE MAIDAN

Tell me where you are now.

The voice in Alfie's head was now a familiar one, even if at that moment he couldn't quite place its owner. It felt as though he was standing on a theatrical stage, and the voice was calling to him from the darkness of the wings.

Alfie?

He was standing at the crossroads of two broad, dusty streets, in the shadow of imperious white buildings that could have been found in the heart of London, amid the dash and clatter of the Strand or Whitehall. But the roads here were quiet, the whole scene draped in lethargy. The sun was low in the sky, a fierce red ball shimmering in the haze. The bludgeoning heat beat down upon Alfie's head like a cudgel. He could only be in Calcutta.

Tell me where you are, Alfie.

"I'm not sure," he replied, faltering. "I went for a walk."

The knowledge was slowly coming back to him, somewhere between a dream and a memory. He had left the house earlier that afternoon, slipping out unseen into the Indian heat. A month had passed since the violent night of the séance, and the Mandeville home had regained its usual stately decorum. Alfie thought he detected a slight stiffness in the way that his father spoke to Stowbridge – the butler's hand upon his master's arm had not been forgotten – but apart from that everything had returned to normal. It was as if there had been an unspoken decision to pretend that nothing had ever happened. That was the problem with his family, Alfie had decided. The Mandevilles were so concerned about only saying things that were right and proper, they never said anything at all. Complaints went stale like unaired laundry. Problems turned rotten and mouldy. Skeletons rattled in closets.

But if a collective vow of silence had been taken over the events surrounding the séance, then one person hadn't been informed.

"What an incredible kerfuffle!" Selena had exclaimed to Alfie two Sundays later, in a snatched conversation outside church. "I haven't seen my father that upset for years! You should have heard him in the carriage on the way home. He called your father every name under the sun. Apparently Lord Mandeville came crashing into the drawing room like a madman, overturning furniture and threatening everyone. My father feared that blood would be spilled."

"It was truly horrible," said Alfie solemnly. "I'm sorry you were caught up in it."

"Sorry?" Selena burst out laughing. "Whatever for, Lord Mandy Vile? It was the most tremendous fun! Whilst my father was huffing and puffing away, Amelia Brockhurst was so het up she could barely breathe, the silly old sow! Serves her right!"

As usual, Selena's laughter made Alfie feel a bit better about the world. The whole situation had made him restless, and Alfie could feel the first stirrings of rebellion within him. He couldn't leave the house without a small circus following in his wake: an *ayah*, a coachman, an umbrella bearer, and a whole flock of attendants whose sole purpose appeared to be stopping Alfie from doing anything he wanted to do. He felt ridiculous, sitting on the back of a prancing pony like some pampered prince. Alfie wanted to climb down and walk about the streets on his own two feet, experiencing the rush and the excitement of Calcutta for himself.

So, earlier that afternoon, Alfie had sneaked out of the house. It had been simple enough – Lord Mandeville was attending an important meeting at Government House and Lady Mandeville was back in bed. Since the séance, Alfie's mother's shades had returned with a vengeance, and she seemed to be taking ever more frequent doses of laudanum. Her expression was perpetually dreamy, and Alfie wasn't sure whether his words registered when he spoke to her. Lady Mandeville had always been delicate and sensitive, the graceful doe beside her fierce husband's white tiger. But the more time his mother spent in her bedroom, the more Alfie worried, as did his father – although whether that was because Lord Mandeville cared for his wife, or simply feared further embarrassment, it was hard to tell.

Once he was safely out of the house, Alfie had followed the broad thoroughfares of the European quarter of Calcutta until they narrowed and began to follow a twisting, tortuous path through the city. In the Indian quarter no two houses looked the same. Meticulously kept houses with verandahs shared walls with shacks and lean-tos. Crowded washing lines sagged under the weight of damp saris and dhotis. The air was a combustible brew of odours, the spicy aromas of the food stalls and the butchers' shops mixing with the sour tang of the rubbish piles by the side of the road.

Alfie walked quickly, ignoring the wide-eyed stares that greeted his progress. British children were rarely seen in the Indian town; unaccompanied, never. But he didn't feel frightened. He found the bustling streets invigorating, the shouts and chatter of foreign tongues mysterious and exciting. Dodging a bullock-cart, he entered the humming marketplace of the bazaar. People had come from all quarters of Calcutta – Hindu and Muslim, Chinese and European – lured by a dizzying array of treasures, from dresses and jewellery to sweetmeats and cloth, rice and lucifer matches. Shopkeepers and customers haggled over the price of every item, turning purchases into prolonged verbal duels. More than once Alfie had to evade the grasp of a smiling storeowner as he tried to steer him inside his emporium.

He was crossing the street to avoid the pungent stink of a liquor shop when he got the unsettling sensation that someone was watching him. When he glanced over his shoulder, he spotted Ajay, the punkawallah's son, slipping into a hookah shop, where the men had gathered to smoke their water pipes. Alfie swore under his breath. Was Ajay following him?

Cutting down an alleyway, Alfie ducked into a doorway and waited. Thirty seconds passed, then a minute, and then Ajay padded past. Alfie jumped out and grabbed him by the shoulder, spinning him around. The Indian boy looked at him calmly, his face betraying not even a flicker of surprise.

"Why are you following me?" Alfie demanded. "What do you want?"

"You shouldn't be here," said Ajay, flicking his dark fringe out of his eyes. His English was heavily accented but surprisingly fluent.

"I'll go where I damn well please!"

"Leave Calcutta, please. And leave India. You are not welcome here. I will take care of Miss Marbury. She will be safe with me."

"Safe with you? You must be joking! Stay away from her, you hear me?" Alfie shouted. "Now leave me alone!"

With a small shrug, Ajay turned and walked away down the alleyway. Alfie waited until he was sure the boy had gone before he carried on his way. This time, he told himself firmly, he really was going to say something to Lord Mandeville about Ajay. He had been as patient as possible, but there were limits.

Suddenly Alfie didn't want to stay in the bazaar any longer. He stomped back towards the British quarter of Calcutta, past the shops and stalls as they closed up for the day. By the time he had reached the crossroads the light was fading and he knew that he should go home, but his run-in with Ajay had only worsened his mood. So Alfie headed south, and soon came out on to a vast expanse of lush grass stretching away into the distance, broken up by wide avenues and the occasional clump of trees: the Maidan.

Part park, part parade ground, the Maidan was the bustling hive at the centre of Calcutta's social life. Alfie entered the grassy common at the north-east corner, where the white mansions of Chowringhee Road met the elegant, tree-lined Esplanade Row. Somewhere behind the trees lay Government House, the home of the Viceroy. Alfie wondered what Selena was doing at that moment, whether she felt as lost and as alone as he did. He doubted it. Selena seemed to have an answer for everything.

Lost in his own thoughts, Alfie mooched along the avenues down the Maidan, past English couples out taking the early-evening air. To his west lay the river Hooghly, and the square-rigged sailing ships patiently loading up on coal, tea and jute. The jagged star of Fort William rose up in front of them. As a son of the British Empire, Alfie knew that he was supposed to find the fort's presence reassuring, but in truth it unsettled him. The original Fort William had been damaged in a siege over a hundred years before, when relations between the British and the Indians had not been at a dangerously low ebb. When it was rebuilt, and relocated to the south, the surrounding landscape had been levelled to provide the soldiers with clear firing lines should they be attacked again. In that way, the Maidan was more than just a park – it was also a warning.

As Alfie continued south, the racetrack of the Royal Calcutta Turf Club drew into view. Whenever his father had taken him to the races, Alfie had been overwhelmed by the sheer noise of the spectacle: the thunder of hooves and roar of the crowd as the horses galloped past the winning post; the heavy clunk of wooden mallets during the polo matches. By now the afternoon had given way to evening, and as Alfie finally turned round to go home he realized that he was almost alone on the park. The carriages had disappeared, and the few remaining couples were moving swiftly towards the exits. As he followed their distant progress, Alfie saw something that made him frown, and suddenly he realized why everyone was leaving the Maidan.

Fort William had vanished, and not through some magician's grand illusion. A thick bank of mist was rolling off the Hooghly River, devouring everything in its grey maw. Alfie tried to pick up his pace, but the long afternoon's walk weighed heavily upon his legs. He felt like a convict dragging a ball and chain. By the time he reached the nearest clump of trees the mist had swallowed up Esplanade Row, and the mansions of Chowringhee Road had been reduced to vague outlines. This was starting to get serious – without any landmarks to guide him, how was Alfie supposed to find his way out of the Maidan?

Trying to quell his rising panic, Alfie continued in what he hoped was a northerly direction. The entire park was now submerged in a damp grey blanket. Tall statues reared up out of the gloom, haughtily defying the fog's ambush. The marble giants looked down on Alfie, seemingly contemptuous of his plight. He cursed himself for being so stubborn. Why hadn't he made for home hours ago? When he turned around now to try and get a sense of his bearings, every direction looked the same. It was as though he was trapped in a giant cell with grey walls on every side.

Just as he was about to give up all hope, he saw somewhere amidst the fog, a light bobbing in the murk like a will o' the wisp. Alfie hurried towards it, praying that it would lead him to an exit, or even just a friendly face. As he drew closer, his spirits rose at the sight of a bandstand's silhouette jutting out before him. On brighter summer days, Alfie would come here with his family to watch orchestras play on the raised platform. It meant he had to be in the north-west corner of the park – and not far from a way out.

But when he looked beyond the bandstand, Alfie froze.

A figure was floating across the Maidan, so pale and vague that it barely seemed flesh and bone, more a spirit flitting across the boundary between this and some other, hidden world. It carried a lantern high above its head as it swept across the park, and appeared to be searching for something. As Alfie watched, the ghost drifted up the steps of the bandstand and stood by the rail. It leaned into the fog and called out, in a high, quavering voice, his name.

"Mother!" cried Alfie.

And, unbelievably, it was Lady Mandeville standing alone upon the bandstand. Dressed in a long cotton nightdress, and with her bare feet covered in mud and grime, she looked as though she had risen straight from her bed. When Alfie waved and called out to her, she let out a cry.

"Oh Alfie, thank God! Thank God!"

Lady Mandeville ran down the steps of the bandstand and enveloped him in a fierce embrace.

"Where have you been?" she said. "I've been so worried!"

"I'm sorry, Mother," said Alfie. "I went for a walk and lost track of time. I didn't mean to frighten you."

"I was having such a terrible dream ... your father and Frederick ... and when I woke up I knew that something was wrong, I just knew!" Lady Mandeville squeezed him even tighter. "Promise me you'll never run off like this again!"

She was trembling, though whether due to worry or

the cold, Alfie couldn't be sure. The frantic way in which she was talking and stroking his face was frightening him.

"You must be freezing, Mother," he said. "Look at your clothes!"

She glanced down at her muddied nightdress, as though noticing it for the first time. "A little chilled, perhaps," she conceded. "I would have put a coat on but I just . . . your bed was empty and you were nowhere to be seen and . . . your father does have his temper, especially when I am in one of my shades, and. . ."

She faltered, and Alfie saw tears brimming in the corners of her eyes.

"It's fine, Mother," he whispered comfortingly, slipping his hand in hers. "We're safe now. Let's go home."

CHAPTER TEN

ILL WHISPERS

When Alfie opened his eyes again, the ceiling of Dr Grenfell's study swam into view. He sat up on the divan, rubbing his face. The doctor was making notes in the chair next to him, his bowed head revealing a small bald clearing in his thinning jungle of hair.

"Do you think that was important?" asked Alfie. "The memory of that day?"

"It doesn't matter what I think," Dr Grenfell replied, without raising his head. "*You* thought it was important, though."

"My mother mentioned Frederick Scarbrook," said Alfie. "At the time I didn't think anything of it, but now. . . Why do you think she did that?"

"I can't venture to guess why she chose to at that moment, but it's no surprise that Lady Mandeville thought of Frederick from time to time. They were childhood friends – rather like you and Selena. It was Fred who introduced her to your father. By all accounts, it was love at first sight."

"What happened to Frederick? My father would never talk about it."

Finally Dr Grenfell looked up. He removed his glasses and began massaging his temples. "Your father and Fred were on safari in Kenya when they disturbed a lion. It went for one of the guides, maiming him horribly. When the hunting party opened fire, Sir Thomas' son caught a stray bullet in the chest. Your father did everything he could to try and revive him, but it was too late. Fred died in his arms."

Alfie shivered. "How terrible!"

"A tragedy indeed, but let's not dwell on such dark thoughts," said Dr Grenfell, snapping shut his notebook. "We are making real progress, and that is something to be celebrated. You may be excused a cold bath today, and I shall instruct Cook to give you an extra helping of pudding. Here at Scarbrook, we believe in the carrot as well as the stick."

With an encouraging smile, the doctor got up and returned to his desk, indicating that the session was over. Alfie left the study – and walked straight into the middle of a loud argument. Maria was standing in the corridor, trying to prevent a scrawny old man from pushing past her. The man's shabby clothes were stained with dirt, and he smelled of sweat and earth.

"I need to speak to the doctor!" he cried.

"You can't," Maria replied brusquely. "How did you get in here?"

"It ain't right," the old man said. "I need to tell him that."

At the sight of Alfie he stopped suddenly, his breaths coming in loud rasps.

"I know you," he said. "You were there too, weren't you?"

It was then that Alfie recognized the gravedigger from Almsworth Church. The last time Alfie had seen him, the old man had been frozen in horror, staring at the ringing bell above the neighbouring grave.

"Harker's funeral, you mean?" said Alfie. "Yes, I was there. What's the matter?"

He flinched as the old man grabbed him by the shirt. The gravedigger's fingers were caked in soil and his fingernails were black. He looked as though he had just clawed his way free from his own grave.

"I came to see the doctor about that poor lad," he croaked. "It ain't right. Lord knows he made a mistake, but the lad deserves a proper rest. The dead ain't asleep for a night like you and me, they're asleep for ever. I don't care what the vicar says, and I don't care how much silver crosses my palm. It ain't right."

The gravedigger's voice cracked with emotion as he repeated the last three words, and he choked back a sob.

"What's not right?" Alfie asked urgently. "What happened to Harker?"

"*I* will speak to him."

The commotion had drawn Dr Grenfell from his

study. He was standing in the doorway, his face like a thundercloud.

Maria blinked with surprise. "But sir—"

"That will be all," the doctor snapped. "Leave us."

He gestured at the old man to enter the study. As he shuffled past, the gravedigger seemed smaller and subdued, and as the door closed behind them Alfie was struck by a sudden, irrational fear for him.

"What do you think that was all about?" he asked Maria.

She shook her head. "God help me, but I do not want to know," she said, making the sign of the cross on her chest. "I hear nothing but ill whispers on the breeze these days. When I went into the girls' bedroom this morning to change their sheets I felt a terrible shiver run down the back of my spine. Even though there was nobody there, I swear to you something was watching me."

Alfie was relieved when, later that afternoon, he overheard Perkins complaining about the smelly old tramp he had bumped into leaving the Main Hall. He wasn't quite sure why he had worried for the gravedigger in the first place. The watchful atmosphere at Scarbrook was making Alfie nervy, and every time he felt that he had taken a small step forward, something strange happened to put him back on edge. For all Dr Grenfell's optimism, the plain fact was that Alfie still couldn't sleep, and the days were becoming just as uncomfortable as the nights. A headache had made a lair deep within

Alfie's skull, where it gnawed upon his nerves as if they were animal bones. His vision kept blurring at the edges and he had begun to experience tiny jumps in time, as though he had fallen asleep for a split second. People moved across the room; objects vanished; conversations abruptly ended. It was incredibly disconcerting. That morning, as he passed by the portrait of Sir Thomas Scarbrook in the Main Hall, Alfie could have sworn he saw the old man's scowl curl into a sneer. He resolved not to tell anyone about that.

Alfie wasn't the only one behaving oddly. Since his ouija board prank had backfired so spectacularly, Travers had retreated into the background, holding his tongue even when Brooke had burst into tears the previous evening because he was feeling homesick. Maybe Travers didn't want to acknowledge what had happened. Alfie knew how he felt. But there had been six people in the parlour when the planchette spelled out its message, and they had all seen the same thing. There was no pretending otherwise.

Although they had fallen out, Alfie had no wish for any bad blood to linger between himself and Travers. For all his faults, Travers *was* a friend, and life was undeniably more interesting when he was around. But when Alfie went in search of him, trawling through Scarbrook's sitting rooms and studies, there was no sign of Travers anywhere. Instead he came across Rothermere sitting quietly on his own in a corridor alcove. The hulking boy was sitting forward on a bench, playing with a small pocket watch. He cradled the item in his fleshy hands as though it were a delicate piece of crystal, or a baby.

"Hello, Rothermere," Alfie said brightly. "Have you seen Travers about anywhere?"

The large boy frowned, as though he had been asked the capital of Mongolia or forty-five times sixty-one. "On the lawn," he said finally. "Walking towards the woods. I waved to him but he ignored me."

"Sounds like Travers," replied Alfie. He plumped himself down on the bench next to Rothermere. "What've you got there, then?"

"A watch," said Rothermere, proudly holding up the small gold timepiece.

"It's very fine."

Rothermere nodded. "It was my father's. Before he fell from his horse and banged his head."

Alfie reached out a hand. "Can I have a look at it?"

Rothermere shook his head.

"Go on. I'll be careful, I promise."

"Leave off, will you!" Rothermere barked suddenly. He snatched up his watch and stuffed it back into his pocket. "Didn't you hear me? It's my watch, not yours. Mine. Keep your hands to yourself."

Alfie watched in astonishment as Rothermere got up and stalked away. It was the first time Alfie had heard the boy say so much as a cross word. *Typical*, he thought. *One step forward, two steps back. . . .*

*

Alfie was inclined to blame some of the tension within Scarbrook on the weather. Yesterday's violent storm hadn't swept away the muggy atmosphere: if anything, the air seemed to have got even more cloying, closing in around Scarbrook like a tightening fist. That night was the hottest yet. Although his bed was underneath the open window and he had kicked off his woollen blanket, Alfie's skin was damp with sweat.

There was a loud rumbling sound from the bed next to him: Travers, sprawled on his back, snoring lustily. He had arrived late for dinner that evening, deliberately sitting on his own at the end of another table and heading up to bed well before the other boys. He was definitely up to something. With Travers, there was usually either gambling or girls involved, and Alfie had the impression that this time it was the latter. Although judging by the looks of hatred Maria gave Travers every time they saw each other, it was nothing to do with her.

A small squeak interrupted Alfie's train of thought. A mouse, he guessed with a shudder. He hated rodents, with their furry, lightning-fast scuttling and their greedy, insatiable quest for things to chew and gnaw upon. The last thing he wanted was one running around his bed all night. He propped himself up on his elbow and peered into the gloom. The dormitory was as quiet and still as a grave.

It was only with the second squeak that Alfie realized it wasn't a mouse making the noise after all. It was Yardley. The little boy had drawn his blanket tightly around him so that only his head was visible, and he was shaking uncontrollably. His eyes were wide with terror as he mouthed a silent prayer.

"What is it, Yardley?" Alfie whispered.

A sudden gust of wind stole in through the window, catching hold of a handkerchief on Alfie's bedside table and hurling it to the floor. Yardley gave out a strangled yelp and sank further beneath his blanket. A prickle of fear ran down Alfie's spine.

Deep in the darkness, the dormitory door creaked open.

No light shone out from the corridor, leaving Alfie's straining eyes to sift through different shades of night for signs of movement. An attendant would have been carrying a lamp; had one of the boys got up to use the toilet, they would have lit a candle. Automatically Alfie glanced over at Perkins' bed, but the sleepwalker was slumbering soundly.

The hairs on the back of Alfie's neck stood bolt upright as a heavy scuffing sound disturbed the silence, as though someone was dragging a wire brush across the floor. Somewhere in the dormitory, hidden from view by the row of beds, something was creeping across the floor. It had to be an animal of some kind, but Alfie didn't recognize its tread – neither the light pad of a cat's paws nor a dog's clumsy bounding, but a kind of laboured crawl.

Across the room Yardley had disappeared completely beneath his blanket. As the scuffing neared Travers' bed Alfie became aware of a hoarse wheezing, like a punctured accordion. He opened his mouth to cry for help, only for a helpless whimper to dribble out. The scraping noise stopped, plunging the dormitory into silence for several frantic heartbeats. Through the darkness Alfie could make out the silhouette of a large shape at the bottom of Travers' bed. It paused, and then slowly turned in his direction. Alfie shrank back, suddenly grasping for his own blanket. Anything to protect him.

He had managed to pull the blanket over his chest and legs when a mottled hand emerged from the darkness by the railings at the foot of his bed, stretching out towards Alfie's exposed foot.

CHAPTER ELEVEN

HEARTBEATS

The hand wavered at the edge of his bed like a pale cobra waiting to strike. His heart in his mouth, Alfie drew his foot back beneath the blanket's folds and then pulled the blanket up over his head like Yardley had. He lay as still as a corpse, not even daring to breathe, waiting for the hand to seize hold of him. The creature edged closer, until the wheezing sound was so near that Alfie could feel a stale breath playing upon the blanket. He bunched his eyes shut, too terrified to look. Seconds stretched out into agonized, endless minutes.

Then, abruptly, the scuffing and the wheezing moved away, and the bedroom door creaked closed again. Alfie didn't move for a long time, his limbs seemingly locked. The air beneath the blanket was hot with his fearful breaths, the sheets drenched in clammy sweat. When finally Alfie summoned the courage to peer out into the empty room, he took a great gulp of fresh air as he gasped with relief. Whatever had been in the dormitory had gone.

"I told you!" whispered Yardley through the

darkness. "I told you that playing with the ouija board was a mistake! *They're* here now!"

"Who's here?" Alfie asked urgently.

"They won't stop until they find him!"

"Find who? Yardley, who are they?"

"The Scrapers!" he wailed.

Alfie frowned. "Who?"

"Twisted hunters from the spirit world. Vicious murderers who feast on those who are awake. We're all in danger now!"

The ensuing silence was broken by a loud groan.

"The only person in danger right now, Yardley, is you," Travers muttered. "Because if you wake me up again I will ram my fist down your throat until you choke on it. Now shut up and go to sleep."

"But Travers—!" said Alfie.

"That counts for you too," Travers said curtly. "You may not want to sleep, but I bloody well do."

He rolled over with a creak of bedsprings, quickly collapsing back to sleep. Perhaps Alfie should have felt better to have his fears dismissed in such a no-nonsense fashion – but he stayed alert for the rest of the night, his blanket tucked beneath his chin, and he knew that Yardley did too.

The next morning Alfie struggled out of bed in a foul mood. He left his breakfast untouched, and snapped at Rothermere when the boy asked him to play cards. The tiredness was making Alfie tetchy enough as it was without the shocks of the last few days adding to his stress. First the shadow boy, then the ouija board, now the creature in the dormitory. . . Was he starting to see things? Just because he was in a sanatorium, Alfie told himself sternly, there was no need to end up acting like a madman. What would Lord Mandeville say if he told him? He'd never be allowed home!

Alfie hid himself away in the rock garden to think things over, warming his back against a mossy stone. There had to be a rational explanation for everything that was happening. He had been experiencing little jumps in time – perhaps they were responsible. Perhaps his brain was so worn down that it was filling in the gaps with strange visions.

Alfie looked over at the statue of the flute-playing boy, his face a picture of innocence. He scratched his head. What about Yardley? He had been the only other boy awake last night, and somehow he had also heard about the ouija board. Could he have followed them to the parlour and somehow controlled the planchette? But what about the hand – could it have been Catherine's, perhaps? Maybe both brother *and* sister were playing some kind of twisted game with him. Usually Alfie prided himself on looking for the best in people. But he was starting to wonder if he was too trusting for Scarbrook, and the complex, shifting landscapes of its patients' minds. He resolved to keep an eye on Yardley and see if the boy was up to anything.

Heartened by this new course of action, Alfie felt his

appetite return. He wandered back to Scarbrook in the hope that he could persuade the cook into making him some toast. As he headed towards the back stairs, the sound of breaking glass from the drawing room stopped Alfie in his tracks. The smash was followed by a loud thud, and an eruption of distressed female cries. Creeping cautiously down the corridor, Alfie pushed open the door.

The drawing room was usually a calm haven, the serene eye of Scarbrook's storm. Not any more. The red drapes had been torn down from the window, and there was a jagged hole in one of the panes where a missile had been hurled through it. Tables and chairs had been overturned, pictures torn from the wall and thrown to the floor. The girls were huddled up in the corner of the room, shrinking away from the menacing figure of Silas Rothermere. The giant boy's eyes were wild, his meaty shoulders tense with violence.

"Time to play a new game!" he declared, cracking his knuckles. "Who wants to join me?"

He snatched up a vase and hurled it against the wall, roaring with approval when it smashed into tiny shards. His gentle manner had vanished so comprehensively it seemed hard to believe that he had ever possessed it. As Alfie stared, dumbfounded, two burly male attendants barrelled into the drawing room, leaping on Rothermere and dragging him down to the floor. The boy swore and swung a fist, catching one of the men with a glancing blow to the side of the head. The air was black with foul curses.

Doorways filled with jostling patients, drawn to the commotion like moths to a flame. Alfie spotted Perkins and Travers looking on, and Dr Grenfell – his tie loosened and gaze unfocused – pushing his way through the crowd. As the brawl rumbled closer to the cornered girls, one of them burst into tears and began clawing at her hair; another stuck her fingers in her ears and rocked back and forth, muttering a mantra under her breath. Everyone looked shocked by the sudden explosion of violence.

With one exception.

"Bravo!" bellowed William Travers, applauding loudly. "Give them hell, Rothermere, old bean!"

"Be quiet, boy!" Dr Grenfell snapped. "You're not helping!"

The attendants had wrestled Rothermere to his feet, and the crowd hastily parted as the boy was hauled from the room. As the melee swept past him, Rothermere's gaze fell upon Alfie. He swore loudly, and redoubled his efforts to break free.

"I'll kill you!" he screamed at Alfie. "You hear me? I'll rip your bloody head off!"

Alfie stumbled backwards in astonishment, narrowly missing a swinging haymaker. He was saved when one of the attendants wrapped a thick arm around Rothermere's neck and pulled him along the corridor towards Below Stairs. As the dark stairwell came into view, Rothermere's expression of hatred dissolved with a fearful moan.

"Please, no!" he pleaded. "I beg you!"

His strength was dwindling with every step, his kicks and punches sapped of their previous venom. Dr Grenfell hurriedly descended the steps to the door at the bottom of the stairwell, where he produced a key and unlocked it. Tears rolled down Rothermere's cheeks as he begged for help, but the other patients merely stood and watched with horrified fascination as the attendants manhandled the boy down the steps and into the gloom beyond. Then the door to Below Stairs slammed shut, abruptly cutting off Rothermere's cries.

"Shame," remarked Travers, who had materialized by Alfie's ear. "Poor reward for such a splendid innings."

"What happened?" asked a shell-shocked Alfie.

"Rothermere got cleaned out at cards again. Only this time he'd put his father's watch into the pot. It's fair to say he took its loss somewhat personally."

"How ghastly!"

"I wouldn't say that," said Travers, with a thin smile. "It's a magnificent timepiece, Alfie."

"But why is he angry with me? I haven't done anything!"

"Ah." Travers scratched his cheek awkwardly. "You see, Rothermere quite lost his head when he realized he'd lost. He was making all kinds of threats . . . so I told him you'd persuaded me to get the watch for you."

"*Travers!*"

"What was I supposed to do? You saw him – he'd have ripped my head off! I knew that the attendants would sort Rothermere out before he could get to you. He's Below Stairs now, Alfie – he's no danger to anyone any more."

Alfie stared at Travers, speechless. With the drama at an end, the audience drifted away from the stairwell, content to return to their games and daydreams. Alfie caught sight of Maria through the thinning crowd, staring coldly at Travers as he dangled Rothermere's watch in front of her.

"And like a magpie, she appears!" he said mockingly. "Bet you'd like to get your fast little hands upon this, wouldn't you, Maria? Don't even think about it. My valuables are locked in my bedside drawer, and the only key resides upon a chain around my neck."

"I want nothing from you, William Travers," she replied. "My world is a far happier place for your absence."

"And mine for yours," retorted Travers. "Especially as I have found a far more fitting companion to while away the hours with."

With a scornful flick of her hair, Maria turned and marched away down the corridor.

Before Alfie could ask what Travers had meant by a "more fitting" companion, the door to Below Stairs opened and Edmund Grenfell hurried up the stairwell. Pointedly ignoring Travers, the doctor pressed a piece of folded notepaper into Alfie's hand.

"I'm running low on some important medicinal infusions," he said grandly. "Go outside and give this to the coachman. Hurry now, boy, he's about to leave for town."

Alfie nodded obediently and hastened away down the corridor. Given the odour of spirits clinging to Grenfell's person, Alfie didn't need to read the note to guess at the precise nature of the "medicinal infusions" required. The more he saw of Dr Edmund Grenfell, the more Alfie wondered whether the good doctor was in need of some medical treatment of his own.

He emerged through the front entrance in time to see a coach pulling away across the gravel drive. Alfie raced after it, hailing the coachman at the top of his voice. When the carriage came to a halt, he reached up and handed the man the note.

"'Ere, what's the delay?" came a woman's voice from inside the carriage. Alfie instantly recognized its owner as Elsie, Selena Marbury's companion. "I promised her ladyship I'd be back within half an hour," she complained. "I can't leave her long, you know."

With a roll of his eyes, the coachman stuffed the note in his pocket and urged on the horses. As the carriage headed down the hill and out of the grounds, a resolute expression settled upon Alfie's face. There was no time to waste.

He sprinted around the west wing of Scarbrook House, cutting through the rock garden and skirting the hem of the lake before reaching the woods. The sun had slipped behind a cloud, and a thin breeze sent goosepimples rippling across Alfie's skin. As he followed the trail up to the ridge, a woodlark trilled mockingly somewhere high up in the branches.

Running most of the way, it didn't take him long to reach the water tower. The building looked as gloomy and unwelcome as ever, poor housing for a common criminal, let alone a viceroy's daughter. Alfie breathlessly knocked on the door.

"Selena?" he called out. "It's me, Alfie. Let me in, will you?"

Although the door remained closed, the sound of faint voices carried through the wood. Pressing his ear against the door, Alfie heard Selena say:

"Do you think I look nice now?"

A girlish giggle answered in the affirmative.

"Are you sure?"

"Simp-erlly be-you-tiful, Miss Marbury," the second girl replied, putting on a snooty accent. "You are the belle of the ball." Her voice sounded younger than Selena's, her accent coarser for all her impersonation of a lady.

Alfie banged upon the door again, louder this time, but still Selena ignored him. He walked round to the side of the tower and peered through a grimy windowpane. The ground floor had been furnished with basic furniture in an attempt to make it habitable: a table and a couple of chairs, a washstand and a bed. Selena was standing over the basin, a pair of scissors in her hand. She had filled the basin with strands of her beautiful long hair, leaving a savage, uneven crop behind.

Her back was turned to Alfie, and she was talking to someone out of sight in a dark corner of the room.

"I'm so glad you visited me," said Selena. "Life here is so dreadfully boring. I don't know what I'd do without you here to liven things up."

"Things are always more fun when I'm around," the girl replied. "Would you like to play a new game?"

"Yes, indeed."

"Then let's find something new to cut, shall we?" Alfie's stomach tightened at the sly tone creeping into the girl's voice.

"Perhaps Elsie has left some paper around," said Selena. "We could cut out some pretty shapes."

"Pretty shapes?" the girl sneered. "Don't be so wet. You want to have *fun*, don't you?"

"So what do you want me to cut, Lizzie?"

"I don't know. . ." the girl said wheedlingly. "You could nick your pretty cheek, perhaps. Or slice your wrist, that might be fun . . . *or cut your throat. . .*"

"Selena, no!" Alfie cried.

He ran back to the front door and yanked it open, offering up a quick prayer of thanks that it hadn't been locked. Racing inside the tower, Alfie dived across the room and knocked the scissors from Selena's hand, sending the two of them tumbling on to the cold stone floor. Instantly he scrambled to his feet, picking up the scissors and looking around for Lizzie.

There was no sign of her amid the shadowy nooks and crevices of the water tower, but one of the windows was lying open, offering an escape route to the tangled protection of the woods beyond.

Alfie laid the scissors down on the table and crouched down by the Viceroy's daughter. Selena's eyes were closed, and there was a trickle of blood where she had banged her head on the flagstones. When Alfie murmured her name, Selena's eyes snapped open, and she emitted a piercing scream.

"It's all right!" Alfie said hastily. "It's me, Alfie!"

"Thank God!" gasped Selena. "For a moment, I thought. . . Where's Lizzie?"

"It's all right. She's gone. What happened?"

"Lizzie's been here all along," Selena said miserably. "Waiting. When Elsie went into Almsworth to send a telegram, she came to see me. Lizzie said I should cut off my hair, and even though I didn't want to I couldn't stop myself from picking up the scissors. I cut off all my hair, and then she said. . ."

Selena dissolved into wracking sobs. Awkwardly putting his arms around the girl, Alfie hugged her tightly for several minutes until her sobs began to ease.

"Are you sure you're all right?" he asked. "I was worried I'd hurt you when I knocked you down."

"On the contrary," Selena replied, with a loud sniff. "It seems there are some benefits to having a numb left arm. I barely felt a thing."

She smiled, and Alfie couldn't help grinning.

"Truth be told, it was all a bit of a blur," said Selena. "Lizzie didn't try and attack you, did she?"

Alfie shook his head. "I didn't even see her. She vanished."

"Of course you didn't see her," Selena said bitterly. "She's too clever for that. Elsie never saw her, my father never saw her. He tells me I've invented Lizzie as some kind of nasty game to punish him. The doctors just think I'm mad. No one believes me!"

"I do," said Alfie, and it was true.

"Really?" Selena murmured. "You do?"

Alfie nodded. He was thinking quickly now. "Forget your father and Elsie and Dr Grenfell. When we're seventeen we can leave Scarbrook together, and I'll protect you from Lizzie. I'll find work – I don't care what kind – and we'll be happy. Wherever you want to go in the world, I'll come with you."

Selena reached up and touched her ravaged hair. "Even though I look like an urchin?"

Wordlessly, Alfie handed her a handkerchief. Selena smiled as she dabbed her glistening eyes.

"If you keep being so kind to me, little Lord Mandy Vile, I may have to find a new name for you."

"How about Alfie?"

"I'll think about it," she said, a welcome blush of colour returning to her cheeks.

Alfie was suddenly aware of the warm brush of Selena's breath against his face, and the rapid pulsing of her heart against his skin. The mood in the tower had shifted so quickly that his head was spinning. Then Selena closed her eyes, and he knew exactly what he

125

had to do, what he had secretly been yearning to do since the moment he had met Selena. Alfie leaned in towards her.

"Selena?" a woman called from outside. "Why is the door open?"

"It's Elsie!" Selena exclaimed, hastening to her feet and brushing the dust from her dress. "You have to leave!"

Alfie dashed over to the open window and climbed through it, tumbling out of sight just as Elsie bustled inside the tower. The companion's bitter complaints of having forgotten her purse died away at the sight of Selena's shorn hair, replaced by an astonished silence. Alfie crept away into the wood, giddy with the delirium of holding his love in his arms, the nearness of her lips to his, haunted by the sound of his pounding heartbeat.

CHAPTER TWELVE

THE SHALLOW GRAVE

The next day saw the sanatorium's annual cricket match, the Frederick Scarbrook Cup, contested on the Almsworth village green between Attendants and Guests. As he trooped towards the pitch with the other patients, Alfie was surprised to see rows of deckchairs lining the green – apparently the promise of a sporting spectacle had been enough to overcome any village prejudice against the players. Even the vicar was sipping happily from a lemonade, his sharp exchange with Edmund Grenfell during Harker's funeral seemingly forgotten.

The size of the crowd did little to ease Alfie's jangling nerves. Though he enjoyed cricket, he was neither a great batsman nor a great bowler, and there were a few too many onlookers for his liking. Still, he hadn't felt able to refuse Dr Grenfell's request that he take part, and it was a perfect day for cricket. The sky was a bright shade of blue, without a cloud in sight, and the weathervane on top of the pavilion stood proudly untroubled by wind. The players' white uniforms were brilliant against the smooth green playing surface.

Scarbrook's contingent of onlookers had gathered at a tactful distance away from the villagers. Mindful of the speech Dr Grenfell had given back in the sanatorium stressing the importance of good behaviour, the patients were doing their best to control their excitement at the impending contest. They clapped politely as the two teams took to the field, and the Guests' team came together for a commemorative group photograph. Dr Grenfell made a show of mock reluctance before accepting the invitation to join them, taking a seat in the middle of the front row. The photographer was shrouded beneath a thick black sheet that muffled his voice as he instructed the back row to move around. When the flash went off with a puff of smoke Alfie was sure he blinked, but there wasn't time for another photograph. The umpires were ready to take the toss, and there was a problem.

"The Attendants are a man short and the Guests have players to spare," Dr Grenfell told the patients. "Would anyone volunteer to switch sides?"

"I'll play for them," said Travers, to a loud chorus of dismay from his teammates.

"You can't!" protested Sampson. "You're our best player!"

Travers shrugged. "Then you'll have to win without me, won't you?"

"Thank you, William," said Dr Grenfell, with evident relief. "If that's decided, shall we get on with the game?"

The Attendants won the toss and decided to bowl, leaving the Guests' team to troop over to the seats by the pavilion to watch. There was a polite ripple of applause as the Guests' two openers came out to bat. Alfie watched with growing curiosity as one of the attendants tossed the ball to Travers to bowl, who turned and marked out a lengthy run-up. He took off his sweater and whirled his arms around to loosen his muscles, his broad shoulders threatening to burst out of his shirt. When the umpire called "play", Travers thundered up to the crease, sending down a furious blur of a ball that flew past the batsman's defensive stroke, missing the bails by inches before thudding into the wicket keeper's gloves. There was an audible drawing in of breath from the crowd. Travers bowled out two batsmen in his first over, and was only denied a third leg-before-wicket by the shake of the umpire's head. Travers glared at the umpire, hands on hips, earning himself tuts of displeasure for his lack of sportsmanship. Despite himself, Alfie was brimming with admiration. It was the fastest bowling he had ever seen.

"Not bad, is he?" remarked Perkins, beside him. "They say he could have gone on to play for England, had things been different."

"He still could, couldn't he?" said Alfie. "He's only sixteen, after all."

Perkins laughed. "Hardly! Cricket is a gentleman's game, Alfie. And William Travers is no gentleman."

As the wickets tumbled, the patients looked

increasingly reluctant to face the bowling maelstrom. Brooke had to be led to the crease practically in tears. As Travers thundered in to bowl, Brooke dropped his bat with a yelp and dived out of the way, only to watch the bowler gently toss the ball underarm into the stumps. The crowd laughed and clapped, but Travers returned to his mark without smiling. That sent Alfie in to bat; he at least managed to deflect a rising ball into the covers for three runs before Travers bowled him with his next delivery.

In the end the Guests struggled to a bruised and dazed forty-two runs. Alfie thought the Attendants would be celebrating, but instead their team spent the lunch interval arguing, apparently over who was going to open the innings. When play resumed, Alfie was unsurprised to see Travers striding out to take guard. His friend seemed determined to beat their team on his own. Perkins ran in to bowl, only for Travers to drop to one knee and sweep the ball to the boundary for four. The next delivery was clattered back over Perkins' head for six, and it took two of the patients five minutes to reclaim the ball from the bushes. Travers took an almighty swing at the third ball and missed it, muttering to himself blackly as he took up his guard again.

The fourth ball was clipped sweetly along the ground towards Alfie. As the batsmen set off for a quick single, Alfie dived to the ground, just managing to stop the ball with his fingertips. Scrambling to his feet, he hurled it towards the stumps at the bowler's end. The ball went low and flat through the air before clattering into its target, sending a stump cartwheeling out of the ground with Travers well short of the crease. There was a second's shocked pause and then the crowd erupted into cheers, Alfie's team mobbing him with congratulations. Travers stood motionless, staring at the stumps in disbelief. He turned towards Alfie as if to say something, then abruptly tucked his bat under his arm and marched off the pitch.

But if the Guests were hoping the dismissal would signal the start of a glorious comeback, they were to be disappointed – the Attendants briskly knocked off the necessary runs to win by nine wickets. As the teams shook hands, Alfie went over to Travers, who was sitting alone outside the pavilion.

"Well played," he said, offering his hand.

"I should never have taken that stupid run," Travers muttered, tugging at a lock of his hair. "I was annoyed because I missed the previous ball."

"Don't be so hard on yourself! You were incredible."

But Travers refused to be consoled, quickly gathering up his pads and heading off down the path back to the sanatorium. With the match over, the villagers began drifting back to their houses, leaving Scarbrook's patients free to mill about on the grass, or stretch out on their backs and stare up at the blue sky. As Alfie got up to rejoin Perkins and the others, the sound of raised voices drew him to the back of the pavilion. Peering around the corner, he was surprised to see the vicar in earnest conference with the gravedigger from Harker's funeral.

"I thought you had agreed with Dr Grenfell not to talk of this matter any more," the vicar said icily.

"I know what I said, but it's haunting me! Night and day, I can't stop thinking about it. The poor boy."

"That 'poor boy', as you call him, was cursed. He should never have been allowed into the graveyard in the first place." The vicar gave the gravedigger a suspicious look. "You did take care of things as instructed, didn't you?"

The gravedigger took off his cap and wrung it like a damp dishcloth. "I couldn't do it," he confessed. "I tried, but I just couldn't."

"What?" hissed the vicar. "So where is it?"

"I hid it where no 'un would find it," the old man mumbled. "Down by the brook."

"You idiot!" The vicar tapped his foot on the ground in frustration. "This will need rectifying, and soon. I am in London tonight, but the night after you will take me to the brook and we will finish what we started. Is that clear?"

"It ain't right," the gravedigger said forlornly.

"What's done is done," the vicar replied firmly. "I'll hear no more talk of it. Now away with you, unless you'd like me to fetch the local constable."

Alfie flattened himself against the pavilion wall as the gravedigger stomped off towards the church. The vicar mopped his brow with a handkerchief, shaking his head and muttering to himself. As Alfie stole away from the pavilion, he could swear he heard the sound of a small bell ringing.

That night, although Alfie lay awake as usual, he was unusually impatient for the others to fall asleep. When finally the room became still, and even Yardley's squeaks had subsided, Alfie rose soundlessly from his bed, pulled a coat over his pyjamas and put on a pair of shoes. As he passed Perkins' bed, the redhead stirred and mumbled something: Alfie waited until the boy fell back into silence before slipping out through the dormitory door.

Scarbrook was deserted, the gas lamps dull baubles, the last attendant long since retired to bed. Alfie crept out through the front door and across the yard, the crunch of the gravel beneath his feet sounding perilously loud in the quiet. It was so warm that he needn't have bothered taking his coat. Scarbrook's windows stared vacantly at him as he hurried past the charred east wing and down the path to the entrance gates. Beyond the gates, he plunged into the woods that surrounded the sanatorium. As Alfie walked along the country lane, he felt a shiver of apprehension. No one knew he was here – if he got into trouble, he was on his own. And who knew what secrets were hidden amongst the trees?

The crack of a twig made him whirl around, his heart in his mouth at the sight of a large silhouette standing in the lane behind him.

"Easy there, Alfie. It's a friend."

"Travers! You scared the life out of me! What are you doing here?"

Travers' white teeth gleamed in the darkness as he smiled. "I think your insomnia might be infectious. I was having trouble sleeping too. And when I saw you get up and creep outside, I thought, *Hello there, what's Alfie up to? He's not going to the toilet in his coat. If he's up to mischief, he'll need his faithful companion W. Travers to cover his back.* So I followed you." He paused. "Where are we going?"

"To the brook that runs behind the church."

"Righty-ho. And what riches will we find there? Pirates' plunder? Treasure chests filled with pieces of eight?"

"I don't know," Alfie replied. "But it's got something to do with Harker, and the vicar doesn't want anyone to know about it."

"That'll do for me."

As they continued down the lane, Travers cleared his throat and began an off-key rendition of a song about an actress with lyrics that Alfie doubted would have met with Lord Mandeville's approval.

"Shh!" he giggled. "Someone will hear you!"

"And which someone might that be? It's the middle of the night. Everyone will be tucked up in their beds. Only criminals and murderers will be prowling around now – and lunatics like you and me."

"I'm not a lunatic!"

"Of course not. That's why you're wandering the

countryside in the middle of the night in search of some mysterious object. It's everyone else who's a lunatic."

Now that he'd recovered from the shock of his friend's unexpected appearance, Alfie was pleased to have company. Travers was a reassuring presence in the winding moonlit lanes, answering owl's hoots with hoots of his own, picking up a stick and fencing against invisible opponents. A completely different creature, Alfie reflected, to the moody young man on the cricket pitch he had seen only hours earlier.

They soon covered the short distance to Almsworth, cutting past the village green and the slumbering houses to the church lane. The brook lay at the bottom of a small valley that ran past the graveyard and continued deeper into the countryside. As Alfie and Travers scrambled down through the darkness towards the sound of trickling water, it felt like they were the only people in the entire world. Alfie immediately began hunting along the stream, hunched over like a Wild West prospector sifting for nuggets of gold. But there seem to be nothing out of the ordinary, no treasures or secrets amongst the rocks and plants. Alfie persevered, following the twists and turns of the brook as it wound through the valley. Travers' enthusiasm soon waned, and after ten minutes of fruitless searching he sat down upon the bank, stifling a yawn.

"As much fun as this has been, all this wild-goose chasing has tired me out," he said. "What say we head back for a couple of hours' kip before sun-up? Alfie?"

Alfie wasn't listening. His attention was fixed on the half-buried object he had spotted beneath a fern on the other side of the bank. He splashed down into the brook, ignoring the chill of the water on his ankles. Travers followed behind him, curiously peering over Alfie's shoulder as he knelt down beside a long wooden box.

"What is it?"

Alfie knew – deep down, he had known all along – but couldn't bring himself to say it. Instead he brushed the dirt from the top of the wooden box, revealing a brass inscription with a name upon it. Richard Harker. They had found his coffin.

CHAPTER THIRTEEN

REST IN PEACE

"I don't believe it!" said Travers. "They dug up Harker and left him here! The scoundrels!"

"I heard the vicar and the gravedigger talking about it behind the pavilion," Alfie said quietly. "I think the gravedigger was supposed to destroy the coffin, but instead he left it here. They're coming back for it tomorrow night."

Travers scratched his cheek. "Well, one thing's for certain: we're not leaving Harker in the hands of those vultures. Put your back into it."

Alfie hurriedly grabbed the back of the coffin and helped his friend lift it into the air. With a grunt as he shifted the weight between his hands, Travers set off up the hillside, heading back towards the lane. The coffin was a heavy, cumbersome object to carry, and Alfie had to keep half an eye on the ground to avoid tripping on any loose stones or tree roots. By the time they had scrambled up the hill and reached the lane, both of them were panting with the effort.

They walked back to Almsworth in a sombre procession through the night. The coffin seemed to grow heavier with every yard, and several times on their journey back Alfie had to put it down to give his aching arms a rest. He tried not to think about the box's contents – the empty husk of a boy, his breath forever extinguished, his flesh and bones condemned to rot and crumble to dust. Travers was wrapped up in his own thoughts, and Alfie knew his friend well enough not to disturb him by asking about their destination.

They crept through Almsworth for the second time in a matter of hours, keeping to the shadows. At one point a cat sprang into their path with an indignant screech. Alfie nearly dropped the coffin in his surprise, just managing to regain his grip with his end inches from the ground. Travers turned round and gave him a warning look, but said nothing. They hurried away before any lights came on in the village windows, heading back to Scarbrook.

As the sanatorium's gates came into view, Travers suddenly veered off the lane through a gap in the dry stone wall, carefully stepping over a small pile of rubble. He led Alfie along a narrow trail through the woods, beneath the shadowy folds of the trees. The trail began to incline, and as they climbed Alfie guessed they had to be somewhere near the water tower. Finally the land levelled out and Travers came to a halt on a small patch of ground beneath a large beech tree. They lay down the coffin with weary sighs of relief.

Alfie glanced around the clearing. "Why here?" he asked.

Travers nodded up at the beech.

"That's where I found Harker's body, hanging from one of the branches. It seems right that we lay him to rest here."

"You want us to bury him? How?"

"With our hands, if necessary."

Picking up a stick, Travers dropped to his knees and began gouging a hole out of the earth. Alfie found a large rock in the tangled roots of the beech tree and pressed it into service as a makeshift spade. Side by side they dug deeper and deeper into the ground, disturbing the night with soft thuds of cast earth. When the hole was large enough, first Travers and then Alfie dropped down inside of it and began scooping out dirt with their bare hands. They scrabbled like animals for hours, until their nails were black and their shirts damp with sweat.

The sky was beginning to lighten by the time they were finished. Carefully they lowered the coffin into the ground and covered it up again. Alfie lashed two sticks together in a cross with some string from his pocket, and stuck the improvised headstone at the top of the grave. His back was sore and he was utterly exhausted. Judging by the rosy streaks stretching out across the sky, it wouldn't be long until dawn. Alfie brushed the soil from his hands and his clothes, then turned to head back to the sanatorium. Travers remained by the grave, his head bowed.

"What are you doing?"

"We should say a few words." Travers tucked a stray

lock of hair behind his ear and wiped his brow with the back of his hand. He thought for a moment, and then looked up.

"Life is hard," he said finally, his voice a soft, firm footfall in the wood. "I understand that. And I understand why you did what you did. And if there is a God, and He is good, then He will understand too. And if you do have to ask for His forgiveness, you will never need to ask for mine. Instead I ask for yours. I am sorry, Harker, truly I am."

Surprised by the sincerity of the apology, Alfie looked over at his friend, but Travers' head was bowed. A gust of wind had whipped up in response to his words, bringing the wood to life around them. Amidst the rustling of leaves there came the sound of a hundred small bells in, a tiny metallic chorus. Alfie and Travers stared at each other in amazement, and Alfie could swear he saw a tear in his friend's eye. The wind picked up again, howling now through the trees, and suddenly the rustles sounded in one breath, saying one word.

"*William.*"

Travers paled.

"*Beware, William,*" the wood whispered. "*They are here.*"

"Who?" he called out, for once his voice sounding terribly small. "Who's here?"

"*They seek a fiend, and they will not rest until they find him. Beware, William.*"

With a farewell whistle the wind died down, and

the trees were silent once more. Travers stalked past Alfie without looking at him. As he hurried after his friend, Alfie looked back at the crossed twigs over Harker's grave, wondering what the dead boy's final warning could possibly mean.

They returned to Scarbrook to find that it had risen with the dawn. The dining hall was alive with the sound of voices, and when Alfie peered around the door he was surprised to see the girls in their nightdresses. They chattered excitedly as they fluttered around one another, delicate white birds in a cavernous wood-panelled aviary, whilst sleepy-eyed female attendants in dressing gowns grumpily tried to quell the din.

"Looks like we're not the only ones awake," said Travers. "What's this all about, then?"

Nearby, Lucy and Constance were deep in conversation with another girl, a frantic edge audible in their laughter.

"Psst!" Travers beckoned towards the two girls. With a quick glance to check that the attendants weren't watching, Lucy and Constance crept over to speak to the boys, Lucy awkwardly smoothing down her sleep-ruffled hair.

"What's happened?" asked Alfie.

"There was a man in our bedroom!" said Constance, her frizzy hair seemingly alive with the news. "I woke up in the middle of the night and I could hear him breathing by the bed."

"William, it was the most terrifying thing!" Lucy added breathlessly. "I thought I might die from fright, I really did!"

"How very melodramatic of you," Travers said sourly.

"Did you see what he looked like?" asked Alfie.

Constance shook her head. "He vanished when I screamed. It was dark, and I was still half-asleep." She paused. "What on earth have you two been up to?"

Alfie was suddenly acutely aware that his coat was splattered and his hands were stained with earth. Before he could reply, imperious footsteps rang out behind him, and Dr Grenfell strode past.

"Alfred Mandeville! William Travers!" he called out. "Follow me!"

In response to Alfie's questioning glance, Travers shrugged. They had little choice but to follow the doctor into a side room, where he gestured to close the door behind them. Edmund Grenfell was still dressed in his nightclothes, with a white cloth cap hanging limply down from his head. Though his dress might have appeared comical, his expression was anything but.

"Where have you two been?" he demanded.

"I couldn't sleep, so I went for a walk," replied Alfie. "Travers came with me."

"Really?" The doctor gave their clothes a critical inspection. "The pair of you look like you've been rolling around in the dirt."

"Alfie tripped over and fell down a slope in the dark," said Travers. "I scrambled down to help him."

"I see," said Grenfell, visibly unconvinced. "And so this disturbance in the girls' bedroom had nothing to do with you?"

"Dr Grenfell!" exclaimed Travers, with mock indignation. "The very thought!"

"Honestly, sir," said Alfie. "We only just returned to Scarbrook to hear about it now."

"Insomnia or no insomnia," Dr Grenfell said icily, "I don't recall giving anyone permission to go wandering around in the middle of the night. There will be no repeat of such behaviour. If I discover that you had anything to do with tonight's disturbance, I will not hesitate to write to your parents. If you cannot respect the freedom that Scarbrook grants you, perhaps you would be better suited to a more restrictive regime. Do I make myself understood?"

Alfie nodded.

"Really," the doctor grumbled, "with guests prowling the halls at all hours of the night, it's no wonder that people start seeing things."

"You think the girls were mistaken, sir?" asked Alfie.

"We've done a thorough search of the grounds, Master Mandeville. There's no one here. The only people unaccounted for were you two. And if, as you claim, you had nothing to do with this. . ."

". . . then the girls must have been mistaken," Travers finished brightly. "Glad to have been of assistance, Dr Grenfell."

The doctor gave him a baleful stare and walked out

of the room without another word. Alfie let out a sigh of relief.

"Typical!" laughed Travers. "The one time I actually do something good, I manage to get into trouble for it. Let that be a lesson to you, Alfie. There's no reward in acting the saint." He lifted up his right arm and sniffed his armpit. "And I certainly smell like a sinner. I'm going for a wash before breakfast."

Alfie lingered in the side room, a troubled expression on his face. Dr Grenfell might not have believed Constance's story, but Alfie wasn't so sure. After all, hadn't he witnessed something similar from his own bed the previous night? Alfie scratched his head, unsure whether he was reassured or unsettled by the news.

He was about to follow Travers back to the dormitory when he glimpsed a sudden movement beneath a foldaway table. Crouching down, he was startled to see a pair of eyes staring back at him.

"Jesus!" exclaimed Alfie.

Catherine shrank back into the shadows at the sound of his voice. The mute girl was sitting cross-legged beneath the table in her nightdress, her arms wrapped around her doll. She bared her teeth when Alfie reached to try and coax her out, and shifted further beneath the table.

At that moment the door opened, and a pensive-looking Yardley entered the room. Seeing Alfie peering into the gloom, he got down on his hands and knees beside him, his face brightening at the sight of his sister.

"What are you doing down there?" he asked. "Are you hiding?"

Catherine nodded.

"What for?" said Yardley. He crawled underneath the table and dragged his unwilling sister out. Catherine buried her face in her doll's hair as she was hauled to her feet. "I heard what happened in the girls' bedroom, but you've got to stay in bed, no matter how scared you are. The Scrapers are circling, and they won't go away until they get what they want."

Neither brother nor sister seemed aware that there was anyone else in the room with them. Alfie might as well have been a ghost. He stood and watched as Catherine reluctantly took her brother's hand, making sure her doll was safely tucked under her other arm.

"Don't you worry about a thing," said Yardley, leading her firmly away from Alfie and out of the room. "I'll take care of you. You're my responsibility now – now and for ever."

CHAPTER FOURTEEN

BEHIND THE BANYAN TREE

Alfie opened his eyes to find himself sitting in a swing chair in the back garden of his family's Calcutta mansion, staring lazily up at a brilliant blue sky. The lawn was littered with hoops and discarded mallets – casualties of an aborted game of croquet. As the swing chair creaked in the soft breeze, Alfie felt as though he were on some kind of ship, drifting on a sea of glorious boredom.

Over on the verandah, his mother's soft voice drifted out from behind the bamboo trellis as she discussed household matters with one of the servants. Her search for Alfie on the fog-wreathed Maidan seemed to have invigorated Lady Mandeville. There were fresh spots of colour in her cheeks, and she sat straighter and more attentively at the dining table. She no longer seemed so distracted, and Alfie had noticed a half-empty bottle of laudanum in the waste-paper basket in the study. Even Lord Mandeville looked encouraged by the change in his wife.

The back door opened and Stowbridge emerged from the gloom inside, ducking his head to avoid banging it on the low doorway. The Mandeville's butler was a tall, gaunt figure, with pallid skin that stretched across his cheekbones like old parchment. The Indian sun had failed to introduce even so much as a hint of colour into his cheeks, and Stowbridge increasingly resembled a walking cadaver. He walked over to the swing chair and loomed over Alfie, blocking out the sunlight.

"Master Mandeville," he said, with a grudging incline of the head. Even though he was unfailingly polite, the butler's stiff formality could never quite mask a note of disapproval in his voice whenever he spoke to Alfie. "Your father has requested that you join him and Lady Mandeville at the Governor's Ball tonight. He requires that you should wash and dress for the occasion."

Alfie groaned. Though he had come to love Indian life, he dreaded the formal social events that the British inflicted upon one another: the dinners and the social calls, the agonizing amateur dramatic productions. Balls were by far and away the most tedious occasions – a seemingly never-ending procession of introductions and dancing. Alfie would have given anything for a fete or a game of cricket instead.

"Come now, Master Mandeville," chided Stowbridge. "Surely you would not want to disappoint your father?"

Alfie shook his head.

"Then go upstairs and take your bath. Your clothes are covered in grass stains."

With a heavy sigh, Alfie got up from the swing chair and allowed Stowbridge to escort him back towards the house, the condemned prisoner with his watchful guard. But as he stepped indoors, Alfie's vision wobbled and blurred, threatening to collapse into a swirl of black.

Suddenly there was another voice in his head.

What is it, Alfie?

"I don't want to remember any more."

Why not?

"I just don't."

Did something happen at the Governor's Ball?

"I don't remember!"

You must, the voice insisted with sudden authority. *Tell me about the ball.*

Hard as he tried to fight it, Alfie couldn't disobey the voice. The Mandevilles' house dissolved before his eyes, and suddenly he was staring out of a carriage window as the grand colonnades of Government House loomed in front of him. Night was falling, and two burning braziers flickered on either side of the front door. Alfie stepped down from the carriage without enthusiasm, keeping a respectful pace behind his parents as they were greeted by the servants waiting at the front entrance.

Inside, in the palatial ballroom of Government House, couples turned stately circles with each other under the tamed gaze of the tiger heads mounted upon the walls. As he peered through the throng, Alfie caught sight of Selena Marbury standing behind a potted fern. Wrapped in a white dress with lace trim, she looked like a delicate apparition – a vague, beautiful dream. When their eyes met Selena glanced around to check that no one was looking, and then mimed an elaborate yawn. Alfie grinned. At least he could rely on one person for amusement. But before he could go and talk to her, his father's hand clamped down upon his shoulder, firmly steering him towards an elderly couple sitting by the edge of the dance floor. The next half hour was an interminable haze of Lady-thises and Colonel-that's, and lengthy discussions about the weather and relatives back in Britain. Though Alfie did his best to smile and be polite, he was itching to escape.

By the time his parents released him from captivity, Selena was nowhere to be seen. Alfie left the couples making their pretty, pointless patterns on the dance floor and slipped out of the ballroom and outside into the gardens. It was blissfully quiet in the darkness, the soft scent of jasmine and bougainvillea carrying on the breeze. Alfie cut across the grass and slipped beneath the tangled awning of a banyan tree, running his hands across its sclerotic trunk. Then, as he looked into the secluded grove beyond the banyan, he gasped.

What is it? said the voice. *What do you see?*

"Selena!" Alfie replied.

The Viceroy's daughter was standing bolt upright in the middle of the grove, her hands pressed against her sides. Her face was frozen and her eyes vacant, her alabaster skin a pale warning in the moonlight. Alfie was about to call out to her when someone stepped out from the shadows into the grove, and the cry died in his throat.

149

Ajay was dressed sombrely, in a dark shirt and trousers, and in his hand he carried a slender metal implement that gave off a dull gleam by his side. As the punkawallah's son calmly crossed the grove, Alfie saw that it was a pair of metal tongs, grasping a small dark lump: a smouldering coal from one of the braziers by the front entrance. Selena's body began jerking awkwardly, as though she was trying to flee but her limbs were rooted to the spot. Ajay looked at her sharply, and her movements ceased.

Alfie, what's wrong?

"There's a boy with her... I think he might hurt her!"

Why don't you stop him?

Alfie choked back a sob. "I'm scared."

It's all right, Alfie. Take deep, slow breaths.

But Alfie couldn't breathe. He clutched at the banyan tree for support, unable to move, unable to tear his eyes away from the grove. As Ajay approached Selena, he shifted the tongs from one hand to the other, careful not to burn her. Then he leaned in and began whispering in her ear. Selena's eyes widened with horror.

"It's not all right!" Alfie insisted. "He's frightening her and I can't do anything..."

Maybe we should go back inside the house...

"He's going to hurt her, I know it! Someone has to stop him..."

Ajay tucked a strand of Selena's hair behind her ear and stroked her cheek. Then, with a small smile, he lifted up the tongs and pressed the burning coal against

Selena's pale left arm. She opened her mouth in a silent, agonized scream.

Alfie. . .

"STOP IT!" Alfie cried out, flinging his arms into the air.

There was a sharp clap, and Alfie's eyes snapped open. The gardens of Government House were no more; Selena had vanished. He was writhing on Edmund Grenfell's divan, fists flailing through the air. The doctor had to hold him down to stop him thrashing about. Eventually Alfie's fit subsided and his breathing became even. He sat up slowly, rubbing his face.

"Clearly a potent memory," murmured Grenfell, sitting back in his chair. "Rarely have I seen such a strong reaction from a hypnotized subject."

"I couldn't bear to watch," Alfie whispered. "It felt like it was happening all over again."

"As far as your mind was concerned, it was. Had you forgotten what took place at the Governor's Ball?"

"I suppose," Alfie said slowly. "It was horrible to see Selena so scared. And I just stood there – like a coward!"

He looked away, wiping a tear from his eye with the back of his sleeve.

"Try not to feel too upset, Master Mandeville," said the doctor. "I think we've finally got to the heart of the matter."

"You do?"

Dr Grenfell nodded. "You saw your friend being attacked, but you were too frightened to help. Rightly or wrongly, you feel responsible. Guilt is one of the most powerful of emotions. It could easily be what's been keeping you awake."

"So you think now I might be able to sleep?"

"Perhaps, perhaps." The portly man took off his spectacles and breathed on the lenses, rubbing them thoroughly with a white handkerchief. "Do you know what happened to this Selena girl after the ball?"

"I have no idea," lied Alfie. "We left Calcutta soon afterwards, and I haven't seen her since."

"Good, good." Dr Grenfell smiled. "Let us hope that the unfortunate young lady has recovered. I'm sure that wherever she is, she's in good hands."

Coming so soon as it had on top of the long night burying Harker's coffin, his latest regression had left Alfie feeling utterly drained. From the foot of the staircase in the Main Hall, the first-floor landing looked miles away. But in the blink of an eye Alfie was back in the boys' bedroom, as though time had suddenly accelerated so quickly his eyes hadn't been able to keep up. It was very disconcerting. At least the dormitory was empty. Alfie didn't care any more whether he slept or not. As long as he could close his eyes.

As he lay down upon the bed, Alfie noticed a small white triangle poking out from beneath his pillow. It was the corner of a photograph, the colours drenched in a wash of sepia: the Guests' team during the Scarbrook cricket match. Dr Grenfell was beaming with pride in the centre of the picture, whilst around him the patients had their arms folded and were trying to look as old and stern as possible. At the time Alfie had been sure that the flash had made him blink, and sure enough he was the only one with his eyes closed. Next to him Travers stared defiantly into the camera, his chiselled features taking on a cruel slant.

As he studied the photograph, Alfie saw that there was someone standing between them – although he was sure that they had been standing side by side at the time. It was another boy, his figure a wispy outline. Alfie didn't recognize him, but the look on the boy's face sent a shiver down his spine. The boy was staring at Travers with murder in his eyes, his face twisted with hatred.

CHAPTER FIFTEEN

THE BATHHOUSE

Alfie stared at the photograph for a long time before hiding it in the back of his bedside drawer. He had no idea who had left it under his pillow, or why. Was the photograph a message? A warning? After all, Alfie looked more kindly upon Travers than anyone at Scarbrook, and even he couldn't deny his friend had been acting increasingly oddly. Travers had become something of a recluse, disappearing for hours on end without any explanation. Since Rothermere had been sent Below Stairs, he had apparently lost all interest in cards – and all other games, for that matter. Whether the events at Harker's graveside had unsettled him, Alfie couldn't say. But the harsh truth was that Travers' absence had lightened the mood around Scarbrook. Freed from the threat of his withering tongue, natural prey like Brooke and Sampson were free to run around and play as they pleased. Perkins made jokes about him behind his back. Even Yardley seemed cheerier.

So when, next morning, Travers suggested that they go for a walk, Alfie's initial reaction was one of surprise – and a little trepidation.

"I'm treating myself to a morning bath, so I'll meet you outside Grenfell's Folly," said Travers crisply, buttering a piece of toast. "Shall we say eleven o'clock?"

Alfie nodded in agreement, and as the Almsworth church bell chimed eleven he walked out of Scarbrook's front entrance and skirted around the blackened husk of the east wing. The morning was bright and sunny, and Alfie whistled a jaunty tune to himself as he strode across the parched lawn. The ground began to slope downwards, gradually revealing the ornate pagoda at the bottom of the hollow. According to Dr Grenfell the pagoda had been built on the express orders of Sir Thomas Scarbrook on the fifth anniversary of Frederick's death, and it remained his most eccentric design. When Scarbrook became a sanatorium, the doctor had converted the building into a bathhouse for the patients. For all Grenfell's pride in the results, the patients could never quite forget the building's frivolous past, and it remained known to all and sundry as "Grenfell's Folly".

Despite having to trudge to the bathhouse every morning for his punishing cold baths, Alfie was fond of the building, which, with its elegantly layered roofs, resembled a giant red wedding cake. He took up a position in the doorway to wait for Travers, but twenty minutes elapsed without his friend appearing. No doubt Travers was lost in his own reflection, Alfie thought to himself sourly. Eventually, with an exclamation of impatience, he opened the bathhouse door and went inside.

Although from the outside the pagoda promised a riot of Oriental colour, inside the building was spare and gloomy. The original marble statues and luxurious reclining sofas had been removed from the main room, and a rectangular plunge pool had been dug into the centre of the floor. The brightly coloured wall hangings of writhing dragons had been taken down and replaced with cold white tiles. There was no sign of any boys, and the girls were barred from the bathhouse – partly to prevent any inappropriate encounters, but also to protect their fragile physiques from the strain of the heat.

Alfie closed the door behind him, shutting out the morning.

"Hello?" he called out. His voice made a lonely echo as it reverberated around the chamber walls. There was no reply.

"Where the devil have you got to, Travers?" Alfie said crossly. "This had better not be one of your silly games."

As he walked around the edge of the plunge pool, his ears picked up a slow drip-drip-drip coming from one of the anterooms. He went over and knocked on the door, but no response came from within. Cautiously pushing open the door, Alfie entered a foggy jungle. The air was thick with steam and it was suffocatingly warm – as though a London pea-souper had descended upon a tropical island. A tap dripped solemnly into a full bathtub, marking out the seconds. The deep water promised a long, warm embrace.

As he strained to see through the steam, a wave of dizziness overwhelmed Alfie, and he had to reach out to the wall to steady himself. He felt a sudden urge to flee the bathhouse and return to the fresh air outside. But what if Travers had slipped and banged his head, and was lying somewhere in the fog?

As he inched closer to the brimming bathtub, Alfie thought he saw a movement beneath the surface. He peered over the edge.

"Travers?"

A hand exploded out from the water, grabbing Alfie by the neck and dragging him beneath the surface.

The water was shockingly, impossibly cold, and far, far deeper than it should have been. As he plunged head first into the depths, Alfie opened his mouth to scream, but the sound died in a futile gurgle and a mouthful of dank water. The hand maintained a vicious grip around his neck, sharp claws digging into soft flesh. Alfie thrashed about, his eyes bulging open to reveal a confusion of movement and bubbles amid the watery darkness. His mouth was still open with shock, his lungs burning even as they filled with liquid.

As Alfie kicked out desperately, his foot connected with a heavy weight. The hand momentarily loosened its grip, allowing Alfie to twist and wrench his neck free. Fighting for air, he kicked himself clear, arrowing upwards through the water. From beneath him came an enraged roar.

Alfie exploded through the surface of the bath with

a loud gasp, his hands scrabbling for the sides. Frantically he pulled himself out, tumbling over the side of the tub as a gnarled, mottled hand shot out from the water and swiped at the air. With a moan of horror, Alfie dragged himself away across the tiles. He crawled out of the antechamber and through the main room past the plunge pool, not daring to look over his shoulder. He managed to scrabble open the front door and drag himself into the sunshine before his strength finally failed him, and he collapsed, half coughing, half sobbing, upon the grass.

In the room Alfie had left behind, the gnarled hand slipped back beneath the water, which continued to slosh around violently for several minutes before finally settling, leaving the surface a serene plain, and the tub an innocent vessel once more.

"Ahoy there, Alfie! Alfie?"

Alfie ignored Travers' hailing cry as he stalked across the lawn, water dripping from his clothes on to the grass. Despite the baking sunlight, his teeth were chattering and he was shivering uncontrollably. He had been walking around the back of Scarbrook House just as Travers had emerged from the woods, a second smaller figure flitting through the shadows behind the elder boy. When Alfie didn't respond to his call, Travers gave chase across the grass.

"Don't pretend you didn't hear me calling you back there, because I know you did," he said pointedly.

"Look, I'm sorry I was late, but I wanted to tell you . . . since Maria and I fell out, I've been spending time with Lucy instead. Only now she's proving tiresomely insistent upon my company, and although I'm a gentleman, it's getting to the point where. . ." Travers' voice tailed off. "Good grief, Alfie, you're as white as a sheet. And you're drenched! What on earth have you been up to?"

"Nothing," Alfie replied tightly, not trusting himself to say any more without bursting into tears.

"Well, *something's* happened." Travers grabbed Alfie's arm. "Look here, slow down and talk to me!"

"Leave me alone!" yelled Alfie, yanking his arm free and hurrying away, leaving his friend a picture of bemusement in the middle of the lawn. There was only one person Alfie wanted to speak to at that moment, and it wasn't Travers.

Cutting through the archway into the rock garden, Alfie found Yardley on his hands and knees amongst the moss-covered stones. Catherine was perched on a smooth shelf, her doll miming an elaborate pantomime as her brother crawled about. As Alfie approached, Yardley emerged from the rocks triumphantly clutching a fat spider, which wriggled in protest as the boy stuffed it inside a matchbox and slipped his prize inside his pocket. Engrossed in his task, he squealed with surprise when Alfie grabbed him by the shirt and slammed him against a rock. Catherine looked up from her doll, her eyes wide with indignation.

159

"Let me go!" Yardley cried, his feet struggling to touch the gravel. "You're hurting me!"

"What's happening to me?" snarled Alfie. "You've got all the answers, haven't you? Tell me what's happening here!"

"You know!" Yardley shouted back. "You were awake – you saw it in the bedroom!"

"I didn't see anything," Alfie said firmly. "Unlike you, I'm not some baby who sees ghosts and ghouls every time he turns around."

"Not a ghost or a ghoul," replied Yardley. "A Scraper. And it's very real, Alfie."

"Stop lying to me!" Alfie shouted, banging Yardley's back hard against the rock. "There's no such thing!"

"I'm not lying!" Yardley retorted, spittle flying from his mouth. "Don't you understand? People are going to die if you don't listen to me!"

"Like your parents did, you mean?"

"Yes!" shouted Yardley. "Just like them! When I said I could talk to the spirit world they talked over me. When I told them I had this constant, terrible urge to light a match and watch the flames play, they pretended not to hear. When I warned them the urge was growing too strong to resist, and that they were in danger, all they did was laugh at me. And now they're dead."

He stared defiantly at Alfie, his wide eyes unblinking. As Alfie felt his anger ebb away, he relaxed his grip and set Yardley down on the ground. Then he slumped on

160

to a rock and put his head in his hands.

"I'm sorry," he said. "I shouldn't have been so rough. I'm just scared, that's all."

"What happened?" asked Yardley.

"I don't know. . . I was looking for Travers in the bathhouse. Something came after me, dragged me into the bath. It was so deep. . . I nearly drowned."

"A Scraper attacked you in the daytime?" gasped Yardley. "They must be *ravenous*. They usually only ever attack at night."

"Stop talking about Scrapers! They don't exist!"

"Oh really? Then what happened to you in the bathhouse?"

Alfie looked away.

"The spirit world has warned me all about the Scrapers," Yardley continued. "They are hunters, nightmares made flesh. They feed on skin and muscle and marrow, and will eat anything that strays into their path. Their eyesight is terrible but they can detect fear like an odour on the breeze, or a taste of food on the tongue. If you want to stay safe, you're best off not even knowing they're there. The best defence of all is to be asleep."

Bitter laughter echoed around the rock garden.

"Well that's just marvellous, Yardley," said Alfie. "Because the only reason I'm here is because I can't bloody well sleep!"

"You can still take precautions," Yardley replied firmly. "I told you, the Scrapers' only weakness is their eyesight. If you see one, cover yourself up in your blanket. No matter how close they get, stay as still as you can. And whatever you do, *don't get out of bed*."

Alfie shook his head. "I can't believe I'm listening to this. If you're so sure everyone's in danger, why haven't you told anyone? Why haven't you told Dr Grenfell?"

"Tell the doctors?" A reedy laugh escaped from Yardley's mouth. "Go ahead and try. They'll look at you like they look at me, and then you'll be sorry. You'll be locked up for the rest of your life."

"So all I can do is hide beneath my blanket until these things go away? What are they doing here? What do they want?"

"They're looking for something. Something very important indeed. And when you played with the ouija board, you let them know it was here."

"Let them know what was here?"

As Yardley looked away, Alfie's mind took him back over the jumbled events of the past few days, until he was back standing alongside Travers by a fresh grave, hearing a warning rustling through the darkness. And then he understood.

"It's a fiend, isn't it?" said Alfie.

Catherine gathered up her doll and wrapped her arms around it, glancing warily around the rock garden. Yardley swallowed and pushed his glasses up the bridge of his nose.

"I don't know anything about that," he said nervously.

"You're lying."

"I'm not!"

"Harker's spirit warned us about it after Travers and I buried his coffin. Tell me about the fiend, Yardley. What is it? What's it got to do with Scarbrook?"

"You don't understand." Yardley's voice shrank to a whisper. "I don't want to get into trouble."

Alfie glanced around the rock garden. "With who? The Scrapers?"

"The spirit world contains far more than the ghosts and ghouls you mock, Alfie," Yardley whispered. "There are creatures of great light, and great darkness. The fiend is . . . an abomination. It is a thing of pure evil, not meant for this world. For thousands of years it was locked up in the deepest, darkest dungeon in the spirit world, shackled and guarded at all times. Only it escaped."

"Escaped? From where?"

Yardley's reply cut like a chill wind through the sunshine.

"From Hell," he said hoarsely. "The fiend escaped from Hell. That's why the Scrapers are in Scarbrook. They're here to drag it back."

CHAPTER SIXTEEN

S.O.S.

There was a long silence as Alfie stared incredulously at Yardley. Then Alfie burst into nervous laughter.

"Travers was right," he said. "You *are* insane."

"Travers doesn't know what I know," said Yardley. "He doesn't hear what I hear. He doesn't see what I see. None of you do."

"But this doesn't make any sense!" Alfie exclaimed. "If the Scrapers are after this fiend, can't we just find it and hand it over to them?"

"How?" Yardley replied simply. "Do you know what form the fiend takes, or where it hides? The spirit world doesn't, and neither do the Scrapers – yet. But they'll track it down soon enough. I told you, they are drawn to fear, and the only thing the fiend fears is being taken back to Hell and locked up again. It can't hide for ever. In the meantime we have to stay as far out of the way as possible. At night, stay in bed, and keep beneath your blanket. And watch out for fire."

At the mention of the word "fire", Catherine's face became a picture of mute horror. The adrenaline was beginning to ebb away from Alfie's system following the events at the bathhouse, and he was suddenly aware of the sopping wet clothes against his skin. He rubbed his face wearily.

"Enough," he said. "Believe what you want. I'm not listening to any more of this."

Turning his back on the two siblings, he walked away down the path through the large rocks.

"Remember what I told you, Alfie!" Yardley called out after him. "Fire awaits!"

The boy's words echoed in Alfie's ears as he left the rock garden and returned to the sturdy refuge of Scarbrook House. He spent the rest of the day reading and messing about with the other boys, determined not to spend another second thinking about Yardley and his wild talk. But that night, while the others slumbered around him, Alfie stayed wrapped underneath his blanket, one eye peeping out into the darkness as he scanned the bedroom for unearthly things.

The next morning Alfie was so weary that he barely registered getting up and eating breakfast. When he caught a glimpse of himself in the mirror on Travers' bedside cabinet, Alfie saw a goblin with bloodshot eyes squinting back at him. The black rings around Alfie's eyes made him look as though he had done ten rounds in the boxing ring. Despite examining his neck for evidence of the attack in the bathhouse, Alfie could find no marks from the Scraper's claws. Did the fact that he had checked and found nothing show that he was still sane, or crazier for having imagined the whole thing in the first place? Alfie giggled at the absurdity of it all, until the sight of his manic expression in the mirror brought him up short.

When he went outside for his morning walk he let his feet guide him, cutting through the woods and coming out by the lake. As he crossed the iron bridge, deep in thought, he spotted a woman approaching from the house. She walked with her head down, but her careful steps were instantly familiar, as was the anxious wringing of her hands. Alfie rubbed his eyes. Could it really be?

And then the woman raised her head, and Alfie's heart sang.

"Mother!"

He hurtled along the path and wrapped his arms around her, tears of joy springing to his eyes.

"I'm so glad you're here!" he cried. "I thought you'd never come!"

"'Ere, get off me!" a voice protested. Alfie looked up in astonishment to see that, instead of his mother's kindly face, Selena's servant Elsie was staring at him, her cheeks flushed with embarrassment.

"What do you think you're playing at?" she snapped.

Alfie sprang back as though he had been bitten. "I'm so sorry," he stammered. "For a minute I thought ... I thought you might have been someone else."

Elsie snorted, smoothing the creases from her

166

dress. "Best we say no more about it. As it happens, I was looking for you. My mistress Selena asked me to bring you a message – not that I approve of her having communications with young men, especially those going around accosting innocent women, but that's a different story. Anyway, she had me tell you that the doctor is having her moved from the water tower today."

"Moved? To where?"

"To another doctor's place in Hampshire. She wanted to say farewell beforehand. She was very insistent – sent me away with a right flea in my ear."

"I'll go and see her now."

"Well, make sure you behave yourself. I have to send the Viceroy a telegram to tell him what's occurring. Apparently the good doctor took this decision without consulting him. Lord knows what Grenfell was thinking."

Elsie bustled away, lost in a cloud of muttering and headshaking. Alfie hurried back over the bridge and up the slope into the woods, his disappointment and confusion at his mistake only compounded by the news that Selena was leaving. As he neared the water tower he heard raised voices – ducking behind a tree, he crept to the edge of the clearing. A carriage had pulled up outside the grim building, and two female attendants were loading cases on to its roof. Dr Grenfell was trying to persuade Selena to step up into the carriage but she hung back in the tower doorway, an unhappy look upon her face.

"Come, come, Miss Marbury," Dr Grenfell said

pleasantly. "I have spoken to Dr Mortimer and he is expecting you today. You will be quite comfortable in his establishment, I promise you. This is for your own safety."

"So you've said," replied Selena. "Several times. But until you explain precisely *why*, I'm not taking another step. It's bad enough that you keep me shut up here like some kind of stowaway – now you want me moved to the other side of the country!"

"We can discuss the reasons behind the move once the journey is under way. But for now you must trust me when I say that I only have your best interests at heart."

"I don't trust you one bit," laughed Selena.

"Miss Marbury, I really must insist."

"Shut your bleeding mouth, will you?"

Dr Grenfell took a startled step back, and the attendants paused in their packing. Alfie's jaw dropped open. Although it had been Selena who had spoken, the voice that had emerged from her mouth hadn't been hers. It had been the same childlike, malevolent voice he had heard in the tower urging Selena to cut herself.

Lizzie's voice.

"What?" she snapped, in the same vinegary tones. "What's everyone goggling at?"

To his credit, Dr Grenfell had quickly recovered his poise. "Nothing, my dear," he said calmly. "We only want to help you, remember? Are you telling us you'd really rather stay here in the water tower?"

Selena giggled. It wasn't just her voice that had

changed – her mannerisms were different too. As though she had been possessed.

"You're silly," she told the doctor, coyly playing with a tuft of her hair. "A very silly man. A silly silly silly fat man."

"There's no need to be rude," Dr Grenfell replied stiffly. "I've been perfectly polite with you."

"You're still silly. A silly fat drunk man."

"I beg your pardon?"

"You've already had a little drink today, I bet." Selena winked. "Mum's the word. I won't tell a soul."

"How dare you!" Dr Grenfell cried indignantly. He turned to his attendants. "The girl's delirious. Put her in the carriage at once."

With a shocking screech, Selena launched herself at the doctor, raking her fingernails down his face and knocking his glasses to the ground. Grenfell staggered backwards, crying out with pain. When Selena lunged at him again, the female attendants grabbed her wrists and pinned her arms to her sides. She screamed, a horrible, high-pitched shriek that threatened to crack glass and pierce eardrums.

"She needs restraining!" shouted Grenfell, holding his bleeding face. "Carver, the strait-waistcoat!"

The carriage door opened and a male attendant climbed out, carrying a white jacket made of thick fabric with buckles and straps running the length of its back. As Selena cursed and threatened, Carver roughly forced the jacket over her head and tied the arms behind her back. He cursed as she spat in his eye, but stuck to his task until Selena was securely fastened inside the jacket. Finally the three attendants were able to bundle her inside the carriage and slam the door shut behind her.

"What shall we do with her?" panted one of the female attendants, straightening her cap. "Are we still travelling to Hampshire?"

"Not while she's delirious," replied Grenfell. "Who knows what she might say? Wait until all the patients are at dinner and then take her Below Stairs. A few days in a cell will teach her to hold her tongue. In the meantime I'll wait here to speak to her serving woman. The last thing we want is the Viceroy meddling in this affair."

The doctor waited until the carriage had disappeared down the hill before getting down on his hands and knees and fumbling around in the grass. Eventually he found his spectacles and put them back on. One of the lenses was cracked, and the frame was bent. With a sigh, Dr Grenfell pulled out a hip flask from his jacket pocket and took a long swig.

Alfie stole away through the trees, his mind a dark whirlpool of thoughts. Selena had fooled him completely – all along "Lizzie" had been a product of her own imagination. The only voice telling her to tear up her clothes and attack her servants had been her own. Alfie knew he should have been disturbed, frightened even, but as he reached the wood's edge his overwhelming emotion was one of fierce protectiveness. It didn't matter what malady was afflicting Selena –

after all, wasn't everyone at Scarbrook struggling with demons of one sort or another? Selena was in danger and Alfie couldn't stand by and watch a second time: he had to help her. Which meant he had to find a way Below Stairs.

Alfie searched Scarbrook high and low for Maria, finally tracking her down in the laundry room. Struggling with a pile of sheets, she looked up in surprise as Alfie burst into the room.

"Alfie? What are you doing here?"

"I need your help. It's Selena . . . they're going to take her Below Stairs."

"Selena?" gasped Maria. "Why?"

"It doesn't matter. It's not safe down there, Maria. Anything could happen to her. I have to go down there and get her."

"But that's impossible! The door's locked at all times, and only Dr Grenfell has the key."

"I know that," Alfie said solemnly. "That's why I need someone to steal it for me."

Maria looked down at the sheet she was folding, and dropped it on to the pile with a sigh.

"So you came looking for me," she said softly. "Because I'm a thief."

"Because I'm desperate and you're the only person who can help me. Please, will you get the key for me?"

Maria shook her head.

"Why not?" demanded Alfie, anger creeping into his voice. "You stole for Travers, and all he wanted was alcohol. I'm trying to save my friend. Why won't you steal for me?"

"It was wrong of me to steal, and it was wrong of him to ask me. Just like it's wrong of you to ask me now. I am sorry your friend is going Below Stairs, Alfie, but I cannot help you like this."

"Then damn you too."

Alfie stormed out of the laundry, slamming the door behind him.

He spent the rest of the day deep in thought, weighing up various plots and schemes. At dinner, haunted by visions of Selena alone in a cell, Alfie struggled to eat a morsel. Briefly he contemplated smashing his plate or starting a fight, anything that could get him sent Below Stairs. But then he would be locked in his own cell, and that would be no help to Selena.

As the afternoon hues of the sky blushed and deepened, the coming of night seemed to only intensify the heat. Even though Alfie had jammed open the window by his bedside, the room remained as fierce and breathless as a kiln. Painful itches swept like bushfires across his skin, from the top of his back to the soles of his feet. He tossed and turned in his bed, unable to find a comfortable position. In the next bed Travers was unconscious, his face as serene and untroubled as a pond in midsummer.

Alfie was rearranging his pillows for the fifth time when he heard the bedroom door creak open. There was a long pause, and then a heavy scratching sound upon the floorboards. Even as his muscles tensed with fear, Alfie found himself slowly pulling his blanket around his body, tucking it beneath his limbs until only his head was exposed. Whatever had entered the room – could it really be a Scraper? – moved slowly, with a hunter's care, down the main aisle between the rows of beds. Glancing to his right, Alfie saw that Travers had turned over on to his front, his right arm dangling out of the bed towards the floor like a fishing line. Alfie had to bite back a warning. If Yardley was right, then staying asleep was the safest option.

Sheltered by the gloom, the unseen creature had reached the bottom of Travers' bed when Perkins sat bolt upright on the other side of the room. The redhead scrabbled through the possessions on his bedside table, then struck a match and lit a candle, the light revealing that his face had once again adopted the blank gaze of a sleepwalker.

But Alfie only had eyes for the Scraper.

It was a hunched figure lying on its side – a figure, but not a man, not of flesh and blood. For, when it turned away from Travers and made for Perkins, the thing appeared to swim *through* the floorboards, one arm arcing over its head and pulling it along, while a back foot pushed off against the ground, propelling it onwards. The entire right half of the creature was lost beneath the floorboards, while lank, greasy black hair obscured its face.

Alfie watched in horror as the Scraper ploughed

towards its prey. Perkins had opened his wardrobe and was looping a tie around his neck by candlelight. Although his stare remained vacant, his face was creased with distress, as if some part of his consciousness knew the danger he was in but couldn't rouse the rest of his brain. With his tie hanging loosely down over his nightshirt, Perkins picked up his candle and headed for the door, light shimmering around him like a halo. In the darkness behind him, the Scraper picked up speed, moving across the floor with a horrible, unnatural fluidity.

"Hurry up, Perkins!" breathed Alfie. "Get out of here!"

The redhead was halfway through the doorway when Travers rolled over and shouted something unintelligible in his sleep.

Perkins started, his eyes blinking open. Alfie tried to shout a warning, but his voice had frozen in terror. With terrifying speed a clawed hand snaked up from the darkness into the light, snatching hold of Perkins' arm. The candle fell from the boy's grasp, briefly illuminating the Scraper as it dragged Perkins down to the floor, wrapping a claw around his mouth, before the tiny flame extinguished and the world was plunged back into silent, terrible black.

CHAPTER SEVENTEEN

THE BEES IN THE CHURCH

Alfie stayed rooted to his mattress for the rest of the night, too scared to call out, his eyes frantically examining the bedroom door for the slightest movement. Seconds stretched out for days; hours lasted for centuries. Over and over again Alfie frantically recited the Lord's Prayer, silently mouthing the words until his lips were dry. He prayed that Perkins would walk back into the bedroom, howling with laughter at another elaborate practical joke. But Perkins' bed remained empty for the rest of the night, the thrown-back sheets an accusation of sorts.

With the arrival of the dawn, the rest of the boys began to stir, blearily rubbing their eyes as they looked around the bedroom.

"Hello, hello – where's Perkins gone?"

"How should I know? Gone to the loo, probably."

"Anyone seen Perkins?"

"I'm not his mother. How should I know?"

"He was taken!" wailed Yardley.

"What?"

"A Scraper took him!"

"A *what*?"

"A Scraper!" Yardley insisted. "It was hunting and Perkins walked straight into it."

"Of course he did, Yardley," said Travers, stifling a yawn. "And what will this Scraper of yours do with Perkins now he has him?"

"It'll eat him," Yardley replied. "It'll tear his flesh with its teeth and gnaw his bones."

There was a second's pause, and then the boys exploded into laughter.

"He saw it too!" said Yardley, pointing a trembling finger at Alfie. "He'll tell you!"

Alfie's face flushed. "I didn't see a thing," he muttered.

Yardley's protests were drowned out by a lusty chorus of boos and catcalls. Alfie maintained a guilty silence. He knew that he should tell Dr Grenfell, but tell him what? That some kind of creature had come swimming through the floorboards and taken Perkins? Alfie wasn't sure he believed it himself. If only the memory hadn't been so vivid, the scratching of the Scraper's nails on the wooden floor so loud as it had hauled itself along. And the wordless horror in Perkins' bulging eyes as he was dragged away. . .

As the patients assembled for breakfast, one thing was clear: Perkins *was* missing. There was a hushed conference amongst the staff at the top table, and as he passed Dr Grenfell's study later that morning, Alfie heard raised voices arguing.

"They haven't called for the police yet," Travers

noted gleefully, as he and Alfie wandered through the Main Hall. "I'll lay you a shilling that all the good doctor's thinking about right now is the reputation of his beloved sanatorium. First Harker dies; now Perkins has gone missing. If word gets out that Grenfell's letting his patients roam the countryside, imagine the fuss!"

Upon leaving the hall, Alfie was surprised to find the doctor waiting for him in the corridor. Perspiration was glistening on the portly man's forehead, and his hands were shaking.

"If I could have a word, Master Mandeville?"

"I'll wait for you down the corridor," Travers offered from Alfie's side.

The doctor waited until the other boy was out of earshot before awkwardly clearing his throat. "A bad business, this to-do with Perkins," he said. "I was hoping you might be able to shed some light on the matter."

"Me, sir?" Alfie swallowed nervously. "I didn't see anything, sir."

"Are you sure? Given your insomnia, I would have thought that you must have seen something during the night. Perkins couldn't just have vanished into thin air." Dr Grenfell glanced over at Travers, who was doing a passable impersonation of someone not trying to eavesdrop on a conversation. "It's not too late, Alfred," he said softly. "Place your trust in science. Place your trust in me. I admit I may have ... underestimated the problem here but believe me when I tell you I am the greatest medical man of my time. I can make everything right again – but only if you tell me what's happening."

Caught off guard by the sudden change in Grenfell's manner, Alfie was tempted to tell him the truth. Then his eyes flicked back to Travers.

"I swear, sir, I fell asleep last night," Alfie said. "I think your treatment may be starting to work."

The doctor looked as though he was about to say something sharp, then caught himself. "Well, that's good to hear, Master Mandeville," he said briskly. "I just wanted to check."

As Grenfell bustled past him, Travers raised an inquisitive eyebrow.

"What did the old buzzard want?"

"He asked me about Perkins," Alfie replied. "I told him I didn't see anything."

"And did you?"

Alfie shook his head. He couldn't even begin to tell Travers what he had seen – or *thought* he had seen. First Selena had been dragged Below Stairs, now Perkins appeared to have been taken in the night by God-knows-what. The only thing Alfie had been given by way of explanation had been Yardley's garbled warning, and he still couldn't quite believe it. All he wanted to do was close his eyes and go to sleep, leave this unsettling world behind and float away on a blissful cloud of dreams.

That afternoon a special Sunday service at Almsworth Church had been planned for Scarbrook's patients. With

Perkins missing, there was talk of the service being cancelled, but Dr Grenfell insisted it go ahead. There was a nervy edge to the atmosphere as the patients trudged down to the village, fuelled by dark jokes and wild rumours. The journey reminded Alfie of the last time he had followed this path, during his midnight search for Harker's coffin. The memory unsettled him, as did the sight of the vicar jovially greeting Dr Grenfell and the patients at the entrance to the church.

Alfie followed Travers to the back pew, where they chose seats out of sight behind a column. The droning lullaby of the vicar's sermon soon had Alfie's eyelids drooping shut, and his thoughts drifted away from Almsworth to another church – St Jerome's, in Calcutta. In his mind's eye, he could see his family lined up in a row: Lord Mandeville, his back straight as a cane, barking out the hymns; the slighter frame of Lady Mandeville beside him, fair-haired, her skin lightly dusted with freckles; and next to Alfie the glowering, ever-present Stowbridge. Around them were arranged the great and the good of the British Raj, perspiring in their starched collars and formal dresses. The congregation was dressed for taking tea on an autumn's afternoon in Whitby or Weston-super-Mare, as though adjusting their clothes to suit the humid climate was somehow an admission of inferiority.

A respectful gap had been maintained on the pew in front of the Mandevilles, marking where the Viceroy and his family usually sat. Rumours were flying around that the Governor's Ball the previous week had been tarnished by an incident of the most unseemly nature. The Mandeville's punkawallah had been beaten and his family driven out of Calcutta, and there was talk that his son had been executed. The respectable denizens gathered in the church were too polite to speculate at the reason, but Selena's absence caused several of the more worldly ladies to purse their lips knowingly. Romantic scandals were two-a-penny in the Raj, especially in the steamy summer months up in the hill stations, but ones involving the Viceroy's daughter – and the suggestion of an inappropriate liaison with an *Indian* – were precious currency indeed.

The congregation was settling into its seats when a sudden clamour from outside drew Alfie's attention to the nearest window. He turned his head in time to see a carriage speed past the window in a cloud of dust, the coachman urging on the horses. Usually the drivers took advantage of the church service to take tea and chat with one another, but judging by the tumult of quarrelling voices, some sort of argument had broken out. Stowbridge cleared his throat loudly, the butler's censorious manner indicating that Alfie should be concentrating on the vicar's announcements. But then a second carriage careered past the window, and a third, and Alfie knew that something was wrong.

A dark shadow gathered at the corner of the window.

The cloud shifted and pulsed before Alfie's eyes, and he became aware of a low and angry humming sound.

Stowbridge leaned in to tell him off, but the words died in the butler's throat as he noticed the shadow at the window. Alfie was nearly knocked from his seat as Stowbridge abruptly sprang to his feet and elbowed his way along the pew. Ignoring the tuts of his fellower worshippers, he raced over to the window and slammed the shutters across it, fastening the latch.

"Don't just stand there, Alfred!" yelled Stowbridge, as he made for the next window. "Help me close them!"

Startled into action, Alfie ran over to close a window, aware of the humming intensifying into a furious whine. Now he understood why the coachmen had fled – the church was being assailed by a swarm of bees. There were gasps as word spread amongst the congregation, and other men leapt up to follow Stowbridge's example. As quickly as they moved, sinking the church further into gloom with every closed window, they couldn't prevent a handful of rogue insects from slipping inside the building, raising screams from the ladies as they buzzed tauntingly around their heads.

While the intruders were easily swatted away, the horde outside refused to shift, laying loud siege to the church. Alfie stood guard by one of the windows, hoping his father would notice his part in the building's defence, but Lord Mandeville's gaze was fixed firmly upon his wife. Lady Mandeville hadn't murmured so much as a word throughout the ordeal, but her face had turned deathly pale and she appeared frozen to the spot.

After a pensive half-hour, word of their predicament

reached the local garrison and a detachment of soldiers hurried to the church to smoke away the bees. When it was declared safe enough to open the doors, the congregation emerged warily into the sunshine, Alfie's mother leaning heavily upon her husband for support. Two days later, Lord Mandeville declared that they were moving back to London. At the time he claimed Lady Mandeville could no longer cope with the climate, but Alfie always thought back to the bees, and their threatening shadow at the window. . .

"Psst!"

Alfie was jolted awake by a sharp elbow in his ribs. He opened his eyes to find Travers grinning at him.

"Much as I hate to wake an insomniac," he whispered, "your muttering was beginning to draw attention."

Alfie rubbed his eyes. The memory of Calcutta had left him dizzy. Dark inkblots were forming in front of his eyes, boring dangerous holes in the grand columns, painting ugly smears over the stained glass windows. The buzzing of the bees had continued even with the dream's end, as though there was an angry swarm inside his own head. As Alfie clasped his hands over his ears, the vicar continued to deliver his sermon from the pulpit.

"As our Lord God has his flock, so Dr Grenfell has his guests, and I my congregation. Together we are a family, who must tend to one another as our Lord tends to us. So let us pray for Walter Perkins, and hope that the Lord brings him back to our family, where we can take care of him."

"Liar!"

Like a slap in the face, the word echoed with shocking volume around the church. Someone was shouting at the vicar. As the patients on his pew turned and stared, Alfie realized, with a lurch of the stomach, that it was him.

"Liar!"

He stumbled to his feet, pushing past Travers and the others until he was standing in the aisle. The buzzing in his head was so loud he had to shout to make himself heard. It felt as though his ears were bleeding.

The vicar was staring at him in incomprehension. "I beg your pardon?"

"What about Richard Harker?" Alfie shouted. "Was he a member of your family too? Did you take care of him?"

"Why, I never met the boy in my life, but Dr Grenfell told me everything had been done to save the poor—"

"You met him afterwards, though, didn't you? After he had hanged himself." A ripple of noise ran through the pews, and two attendants lumbered hastily from their seats. "Did you take care of Harker then? Or did you throw his body out of your precious graveyard and leave it to rot in the middle of nowhere?"

The ripple had become an uproar. As the attendants closed in on him, Alfie was aware of a strong hand pulling him away.

"Step back now, Alfie," Travers said quietly. "It's all right."

"I want him to ADMIT IT!" Alfie bellowed.

"And it does you credit, but you will not make anyone do anything like this. Do you want to end up Below Stairs? Look at Grenfell's face!"

The portly doctor had stood up from the first pew, his face purple with rage. He gestured angrily at the attendants, only for Travers to raise his hand in a plea to stop them.

"I must apologize for my friend, vicar," he called up to the pulpit. "He hasn't slept properly for some months and I fear he's delirious from weariness. May I take him outside in the hope that the fresh air will revive him?"

The vicar nodded quickly, clearly relieved that someone was taking charge of the situation. Keeping a firm grip on Alfie's arm, Travers escorted him down the aisle and out through the doors into the sunlight. The attendants followed in their wake, several wary paces behind.

On the church steps a wave of dizziness crashed into Alfie, knocking him from his feet. He fell to the ground with a moan. The buzzing in his ears swelled to a crescendo before stopping with a loud pop. Alfie looked around him uncertainly. Travers was staring at him in astonishment.

"What the hell were you doing in there?" he asked.

"I don't know!" Alfie said miserably. "There was this awful buzzing in my head and I..." He broke down in tears. "You have to help me, Travers! I think I'm going mad!"

CHAPTER EIGHTEEN

BLIND MAN'S BUFF

While the rest of the patients walked back to Scarbrook, Alfie was ordered to travel in Dr Grenfell's carriage, a burly attendant on either side of him. The doctor sat opposite him, visibly seething.

"I'm extremely disappointed in you, Master Mandeville," he harrumphed. "After all Scarbrook has done for you, you repay us with public humiliation. I shall never be able to set foot in that church again after your lies."

"It was the truth!" Alfie retorted. "The vicar had Harker's coffin dug up, and he would have destroyed it if Travers and I hadn't got there first. You have to believe me!"

"You've been listening to that wretched gravedigger, haven't you?" Dr Grenfell shook his head. "Master Mandeville, as you grow up you will learn that not everyone can be presumed to possess the same level of honesty and reliability. I spoke to the vicar and he told me that Harker's coffin was removed at the request of the boy's family. They had a belated change of heart, and wished Richard to be buried in the family plot. Any other suggestions are just malicious fantasies. One cannot take a gravedigger's word over a vicar's, in the same way that – if you'll forgive me – one would not take a patient's over a doctor's."

"I'll show you if you don't believe me!" persisted Alfie. "I'll show you where we buried Harker's coffin!"

"Enough!" snapped the doctor. "I hear any more nonsense on the matter, and you'll be spending the night Below Stairs."

Grenfell settled back in his seat, staring moodily out of the window. But to Alfie's surprise, that was the end of the rebuke. He was allowed to eat with the others that evening, and no one appeared to drag him away for punishment. Then again, it wasn't as if this was the first outrageous outburst the staff of Scarbrook had heard. Hardly a week went by without one of the patients claiming to be Jack the Ripper's son, or the queen's illegitimate granddaughter. The fact that Alfie was telling the truth didn't make a jot of difference. And as Travers pointed out, punishing Alfie would only have drawn more attention to a matter Dr Grenfell would rather no one was thinking about at all.

Worse than any official punishment was the reaction of the other patients. At lunch Sampson and Brooke gave Alfie a wide berth, as if sitting by him might arouse suspicions that they believed him – or that they were as mad as he was. Sick of their fearful glances, Alfie pushed his plate away and went up to the dormitory, where he retrieved the photograph of the patients' cricket team from his drawer. He felt sure that the strange events at Scarbrook were somehow linked, and that the mysterious boy in the photograph was at the heart of the mystery. Once again Alfie was struck by the sheer malevolence on the boy's face as he glared at Travers. Like the face of a devil. . .

A thought hit Alfie with an electrifying jolt, and suddenly he knew who he had to talk to. He found Yardley in the library, leafing through a book while his sister lay curled up in a ball in the window seat, her doll nestling in the crook of her arm. She didn't stir as Alfie entered the room; Yardley looked up and closed his book. As usual, the boy's wide eyes seemed to suggest that he had been expecting Alfie – that nothing in this world could surprise him. Putting a finger to his lips, he got up quietly and moved over to a bookcase, away from his sleeping sister.

"I don't want to wake Catherine up," he whispered. "She'll only tell me off."

Alfie scratched his head. "Tell you off? I thought she didn't speak?"

"She doesn't speak to *you*," corrected Yardley. "I hear her all the time."

"Are you the only one she talks to?"

"It's for the best," said Yardley. "You know what girls are like – don't want her running around telling tales."

Alfie pressed the photograph into the boy's hand.

187

"Take a look at this," he said urgently. "Someone left it for me under my pillow three days ago."

Yardley examined the photograph, smoothing out the creases at its edges. "It's the cricket team from the Frederick Scarbrook Cup."

"With one important addition," said Alfie, pointing at the angry figure on Travers' shoulder. "Recognize him?"

Yardley nodded slowly.

"I knew it!" hissed Alfie. "It's the fiend, isn't it? The one the Scrapers are looking for!"

"No it's not," Yardley said softly.

"What? Are you sure?"

"Alfie, it's Harker."

"But that's impossible! This was only taken days ago!"

"Impossible?" A glimmer of amusement flitted across Yardley's face. "After everything that's happened here, you can still say that? I told you that Harker was a restless soul. Who knows what a camera can see that we don't?"

"Harker looks like he hates Travers."

"He had good reason to."

"What do you mean?"

"You may count Travers as a friend, Alfie, but no one else at Scarbrook would say the same," Yardley told him. "The moment Harker arrived here Travers saw that he was sensitive, and he bullied him mercilessly from then on. Harker couldn't do anything without Travers mocking him or needling him. A couple of times I saw him with a black eye – Harker was too scared to say anything, but we all knew how he'd got it."

"But if Travers was so horrid to him, why did he go to his funeral? And why did he help me find his coffin?"

Yardley shrugged. "Perhaps he felt bad. If anyone was responsible for Harker's death, it was him. Harker may have hanged himself, but it was Travers who put the noose around his neck. I'm sorry, Alfie, but it's the truth."

Catherine stirred in her sleep, making a small mewling noise. With a caring glance over at his sister, Yardley wordlessly handed Alfie back the photograph and returned to the book at his table.

Later that afternoon, the patients gathered on the back lawn for a game of blind man's buff. The temperature had cooled a notch since midday, but weeks of merciless sun had left ugly cracks developing in the earth beneath the parched grass. Unsure whether he'd be welcomed by the others, Alfie watched from a distance, a pensive outline beneath the shade of an apple tree. To his surprise, it was William Travers who stepped forward and volunteered to be "it" first. A faint smile played upon Travers' lips as a girl tied a blindfold around his head. He was spun several times, the others spreading out around him like strewn flower petals. Then the game began.

Mock-growling like a monster, Travers lunged

forward with his arms outstretched. The boys stayed well clear, only daring to mock and catcall Travers when they were well out of arm's reach. It was the girls who came in close, shrieking with shock and delight at his proximity. The onlooking Alfie realized that he was part of an elaborate charade: just as Travers pretended to be a monster, the girls were pretending that they didn't want to be caught. The gaunt figure of Lucy Albright scurried breathlessly past Alfie, desperate to put herself within the monster's grasp. But Travers pointedly ignored her screams and giggles, making no effort to grab her despite Lucy's repeated attempts to tempt him closer.

"I smell tasty human treats!" he roared theatrically.

"You're getting warmer, William!" Lucy cried.

"I'll need a tastier treat than that."

"But I'm right here!"

She ran straight into his path, nearly knocking them both from their feet in a tangle of limbs.

"For pity's sake, girl!" Travers ripped off his blindfold and threw it to the ground. "Didn't you hear me? I want a proper meal, not your scrawny mess of bones."

Smiles froze; laughter died in throats. Lucy's face collapsed, and she hurtled away across the grass in floods of tears.

"You animal!" yelled Constance. She ran up to Travers and beat her fists upon his chest. "How could you say that to her? How could you?"

Travers didn't flinch. He looked utterly unmoved.

"She was starting to annoy me," he said slowly.

Alfie was about to intercede when a flash of white made him stop and turn. Shielding his eyes from the sun, he looked in the direction of the lake. A small figure in a white smock was walking along the path: Catherine, Yardley's sister. As Alfie watched, she stopped by the edge of the lake, set her doll down upon a bench and then stepped tentatively into the shallows. The sound of Constance's tirade faded into the background as Alfie watched Catherine take another small but deliberate step forward. Scarbrook's patients were forbidden from swimming in the lake, warned off by tales of malevolent weeds clutching at ankles and dragging patients under. But Catherine gave no indication that she was thinking of swimming. She took another pace forward, sinking deeper into the lake. The water was already lapping around her waist – two or three more steps, and it would be closing in over her head.

Alfie began sprinting down the lawn towards the lake, calling out Catherine's name. From behind him he heard Yardley cry out and come stumbling after him, but Alfie's legs were longer and he quickly outstripped the other boy. Catherine didn't respond to their shouts, appearing completely absorbed in her progress through the water. Alfie reached the lakeside path and plunged into the lake after her, the icy water clawing at his heart and buffeting the breath from his lungs. He could feel the weeds at his feet as he waded ever deeper. Startled fish darted away in orange and silver glimmers.

Catherine had come to a stop with the water nearly up to her shoulders. She reached down into the lake, water brushing her cheek as she tipped her head to one side.

"Stop!" Alfie cried. "What are you doing?"

Turning her large, sad eyes upon him, Catherine straightened up. As Alfie drew closer, he saw that she was clutching something; some pebbles, and a thin strap of material. Wordlessly, she handed the bundle to Alfie. He recognized the strap as the tie the sleepwalking Perkins had put on the night he disappeared. And the pebbles weren't really pebbles at all. They were eyeballs.

They turned their sightless, milky gaze upon Alfie as he stared at them in horrified disbelief. It was several seconds before he could regain control of his muscles and move again. When he turned around, he saw that the other patients had formed a concerned crowd at the lake's edge, the previous argument momentarily forgotten.

"What are you doing, Alfie?" Travers shouted. "Get out of there!"

Too stunned to speak, Alfie waded out of the lake and tipped the tie and the eyeballs into Travers' hand. There were screams of fright from both the girls and the boys. Constance fainted. As the patients turned tail and fled from the lake, Sampson fell to his knees and vomited on to the path.

"My God, Alfie!" Travers said quietly. With a shudder, he dropped the eyeballs to the ground.

Amidst the confusion, Catherine calmly waded back

towards the shallows, where her brother helped her out of the lake.

"What happened in the bathhouse," Yardley told Alfie. "The spirit world was trying to tell you something. But you never listen, do you?"

He waited for Catherine to retrieve her doll from the bench before wrapping a tender arm around her and escorting her back up towards the looming outline of Scarbrook House. Travers wheeled away and headed for the rock garden on his own, whilst Alfie helped revive Constance and carry her away. Perkins' eyeballs lay where Travers had dropped them, alongside their owner's sodden tie.

CHAPTER NINETEEN

THE CLOUD

It was a sparse, skittish crowd who appeared for the evening meal. Many of the patients had retired to their beds with shock – several under the influence of heavy sedation – and one girl who couldn't stop screaming was hastily smuggled Below Stairs. The others crept into the dining room, in pairs or larger groups, alert as mice for the sound of predators in the shadows. They found almost the entire staff absent from the top table, most notably Dr Grenfell, amid rumours of an emergency conference in the auditorium.

Talks of a different nature were taking place amongst the patients in the dining room. Those who had missed the grisly discovery at the lake shivered and clasped hold of one another as they were told what had happened, each new narrator seizing the opportunity to embellish the tale with gory details. The largest crowd had gathered at the bottom end of the dining table, where it formed a respectful court around a grubby, unlikely king: Yardley. Relishing his newfound position at the centre of attention, and with Catherine listening impassively by his side, the little boy repeated the warnings he had given Alfie. His words were passed along the table and around the room, chanted softly like a teasing playground song:

> *"The Scrapers will get you if you're awake,*
> *It's the fiend they're after, that's who they want,*
> *Stay in bed if you want to stay safe,*
> *It's the fiend they're after, that's who they want."*

The lone dissenting voice was predictably provided by William Travers, who rolled his eyes as he dissected his trout.

"Utter rot!" he scoffed. "If you listen to a word Yardley says, then you're as mad as he is. Forget all this talk of Scrapers, and fiends, and Hell. What happened to Perkins was a dreadful business, no mistaking it, but there's got to be a rational explanation. Question the servants and the local villagers and you'll find some sort of drunk or ne'er-do-well who ambushed Perkins when he went sleepwalking. That gravedigger, for example. I'll bet you he hasn't got an alibi. Scrapers indeed!"

There was something almost magnificent about Travers' scorn. After all, he had received the warning at Harker's graveside, and had felt Perkins' eyeballs in the palm of his hand. Was Travers too frightened to admit that something was terribly wrong at Scarbrook? Whether Yardley's dire tales were the product of his twisted imagination or not, there was surely more afoot than drunken ne'er-do-wells.

Alfie looked up to find Travers irritably studying him.

"Please don't tell me that you believe any of this poppycock?"

"No, of course not," Alfie replied hurriedly. "It's just difficult to be certain about what happened, that's all."

"Difficult to be certain about what happened?" Travers removed his knife from the trout's innards and pointed it at Alfie. "I'll tell you what," he said, punctuating every word with a stab of his knife. "If one of these bogeymen pops up in the middle of the night and carts me off to Hell, I'll concede that you were right. Until that moment, I'd appreciate it if everyone stopped twittering on like hysterical fishwives. You're in danger of giving me a headache."

Alfie was saved from replying by the appearance of Edmund Grenfell through a side door. The doctor's face was drawn and haggard, his stride drained of all its spring and certainty. He walked slowly to the front of the room and rapped on the table with a glass for silence.

"As you no doubt will all be aware," he said solemnly, "there has been a terrible accident involving one of our guests. We are still trying to ascertain what exactly happened to Walter Perkins, but rest assured we shall get to the bottom of this distressing affair. There is no need for anyone to fear for their own safety, and I would ask you all to remain as calm as possible. To ensure order and decorum, I have placed a temporary stop on all mail leaving Scarbrook. Wild speculations and panic will do none of us any good, and I will not have your parents worried unnecessarily. A Magistrates' Committee will be visiting us in the next few days to inspect the premises. In the meantime, should any of you have any information regarding Perkins' death, it is of paramount importance that you share it with us. I cannot stress that point too forcibly."

The room – which seconds before Grenfell's entrance had been alive with talk of fiends and Scrapers – fell into a determined silence. As Dr Grenfell scanned the tables, spectacles glinting, his gaze seemed to linger over Alfie and Travers. Feeling suddenly and inexplicably guilty, Alfie looked down at his plate and didn't raise his head until the doctor shook his head with weary acceptance and trudged out of the dining hall.

"A terrible accident?" Alfie repeated disbelievingly. "What can he think has happened?"

"It's simple," replied Travers. "Perkins took his eyeballs out to give them a wash, dropped them, and they rolled into the lake."

"It had to be murder!"

"I know that, and you know that, and so does Grenfell. He's stalling for time. An accident's one thing; murder quite another. He needs to get his story straight before this Magistrates' Committee arrives – and if possible find someone to blame. Otherwise he's got some awfully difficult questions to answer."

As the staff continued their arguments in the auditorium, that evening the patients were left alone to do as they pleased. Death had sprinkled the atmosphere with a giddy spice. Those who dared to stay up danced and careered through the halls in a grotesque carnival, jumping out at one another and screaming "Surprise!" When night encroached upon the sanatorium, the mood turned hysterical – the laughter became more desperate, glances more fearful. As the boys changed for bed, Travers slammed his book down on his bedside table, making half of the room yelp with fright.

"Imbeciles, the lot of you," Travers declared scornfully. Turning on Yardley, he added: "I'm blaming you for this, you wretched little freak."

Yardley sank deeper beneath his blanket, his eyes fixed warily on his accuser.

As everyone settled down to sleep, Alfie bunched his eyes shut. In the past he had been jealous of the other boys' ability to fall asleep, but now his envy was tinged with fear. The longer he lay awake, the more danger he was in. Yet the more Alfie wanted to sleep, the tighter his muscles tensed, and the more breathlessly his mind raced. His one consolation was that he was no longer alone. Judging by the sighs and sniffs, the tremulous whimpers, Perkins' death had given several others problems sleeping.

Not long after the lights had been turned out, there was a piercing scream and a stampede of feet along the landing. The boys murmured fearfully and pulled their blankets up to their chins, and there were frightened shouts when the door opened. An attendant appeared carrying a candle, bringing news of a false alarm in the girls' dormitory. Anyone else caught disturbing the peace, the man warned with a glare, could expect a trip Below Stairs. The room seemed strangely calmed by this admonition, and as the door closed once more and the light disappeared the whimpers began to die down.

Alfie remained awake even as the rest succumbed to nervous exhaustion, his mind filled with thoughts of Selena. The discovery in the lake had only sharpened his desire to go Below Stairs and check that she was safe, but for the life of him he couldn't think of a way to get around the locked door at the bottom of the stairwell. In the next bed Travers had tossed his blanket to one side and slumbered with his arms and legs exposed, as though daring any creature to attack him. Further down the row Alfie could hear the sound of trickling liquid, and someone quietly crying. At first he assumed that Sampson had wet himself again, until he realized that it was Brooke who was sobbing. Too scared to get out of bed to use the toilet, Alfie guessed. He would have offered some consoling words, but he couldn't take the risk of waking the others and putting them in potential danger. So instead Alfie pulled up the covers and silently listened to the sound of Brooke's tearful lament.

The next morning found the inhabitants of Scarbrook House crotchety and bleary-eyed. With many of the patients exhausted but unwilling to risk their chance of evening sleep by catnapping during the daytime, the sanatorium was eerily subdued. There was talk that it could be another week until the Magistrates' Committee arrived at the sanatorium. Gruesome tales sprung up that Perkins' eyeballs had gone missing, and were now rolling around the corridors like marbles in the playground.

Everyone seemed to be dreading bedtime, and when night fell the attendants had to physically herd the patients towards the dormitories. They passed Maria as she hurried down the staircase – Travers mockingly lifted an imaginary hat in greeting but she didn't deign to look at him or Alfie. With her head held proudly high, and the dusky tones of her skin deepening in the lamplight, Maria looked more magnificent than ever. Back in the boys' dormitory, Alfie noticed his bedside drawer was slightly ajar, and slid it open to find a heavy iron key resting on top of a notepad. He had to resist the urge to shout out in triumph. Maria had decided to help him after all. Now he could go Below Stairs.

But as he lay in bed clutching the key, waiting for the others to fall asleep, Alfie realized that the gift was a double-edged sword. To reach his destination he would have to risk a journey through Scarbrook at night – and whatever Scrapers lay in wait. Even if he survived unscathed, who knew what horrors lay in store for him Below Stairs? It took Alfie hours to summon the courage to move, drawing on every scrap of bravery and determination within him. Finally, having scanned the bedroom floor for any unfamiliar silhouettes, he lifted off his blanket and crept out of bed. A sudden thought made him pick up a stubby candle and match from his bedside table and slip them into his pocket. He might be grateful for a light in the dark hallways that lay beyond the dormitory door.

"What are you doing, Alfie?" whispered Yardley from his bed. "It's not safe!"

Alfie pressed a finger against his lips and stole towards the door. Outside in the deserted corridor, his bare feet cold upon the wooden floorboards, he headed for the main staircase. He tiptoed down the steps and made his way into the drawing room, only to duck back into the shadows at the sound of footsteps. Alfie drew back behind a cabinet as Edmund Grenfell appeared in the doorway. The doctor leaned against the frame, pinching the bridge of his nose with his forefingers, before weaving an unsteady path in the direction of his study, leaving a murky fug of alcohol in his wake. Alfie waited until the doctor was out of sight before heading in the opposite direction towards Below Stairs.

The stairwell looked even more ominous by night than it did in the day, but by that point Alfie had come so far he wasn't sure he could face the journey back. He rushed down the steps into the darkness and slipped the iron key into the lock. When he turned the key the mechanism gave a loud clank that echoed around the stairwell. Alfie froze, waiting for a shout or a cry of alarm to go up. When the corridor stayed quiet, he took a deep breath and opened the door.

Given all the gruesome tales he had heard about Below Stairs, Alfie was relieved to be confronted with nothing more threatening than a long underground passageway with thick stone walls. He had no need to reach for his candle and match – gas lamps were hung at intervals along the walls, lightening the gloom. Stepping into the corridor, Alfie shivered as an icy draught sliced through his thin nightshirt. Hot as the night was elsewhere in Scarbrook, underground there was a chill in the air. As Alfie continued along the passageway, he saw a row of iron doors built into the left-hand wall – cells, he guessed. All he had to do was work out which one Selena was in. Easier said than done.

Alfie was considering the problem when, from further down the corridor, he heard a girl scream.

Immediately he sprinted past the cells, ignoring the moans and catcalls that had answered Selena's cry. The passageway split into two, one branch leading to a door, and the other to a spiral staircase. Spurred on by a second piercing scream, Alfie clattered up the staircase, coming out into a dingy room that was little more than a row of seats facing a long curtain. When he pulled it back, he found himself looking down through a window upon a sparse, brightly lit room with whitewashed walls. It was a surgery with a long operating table in the centre of the room, flanked by a pair of wheeled trolleys bearing an array of gleaming metal implements. There were three attendants in the room: two burly men – one with a torn sleeve and scratch marks on his face – and a woman, who appeared to be in charge. Elsie was standing near the door, dismay written all over her face. Selena Marbury was tied down to the operating table, thick leather straps around her wrists. A gag had worked loose from her mouth, and she was wailing loudly.

"Please let me go!" she cried. "Please, I beg you!"

"Quiet now," the female attendant warned her. "We've heard quite enough from you for one night."

"Elsie?" Selena twisted her head around, trying to make eye contact with her companion. The pitiful note in her voice broke Alfie's heart. "Dear Elsie, please tell them to let me go. My father would not want this."

"You father wouldn't want you acting so rough, neither," Elsie replied. "The doctor told you he'd have to restrain you if you hurt anyone again. Maybe it's for the best, my love."

"*I said, let me go!*" Selena began thrashing about on the table, hatred festering in her eyes. Her voice had thickened and curdled, and when she spoke again it was Lizzie's voice Alfie heard. "Let me go or I'll beat you till you're black and blue!"

"Where's that blasted doctor gone?" Elsie shouted at the attendants. "The girl needs help!"

"He needed to fetch his glasses," the wounded man replied.

"He's gone to sober up, more like it!" Elsie snapped. "He reeks of alcohol!"

Abruptly, Selena stopped thrashing. Her head snapped around to face Elsie; a glassy baleful look came over her.

"Save your breath," she said evenly. "You're going to need it when I'm free."

Elsie gasped. "Whatever do you mean, child?"

"Don't listen to her," said the female attendant, drawing the serving woman away. "She's delirious. We'll give her something to calm her nerves." She picked up a syringe from the tray of implements and turned to the attendants. "Can you keep her as still as possible, please?"

But as the male attendant grasped hold of Selena, he moaned and stumbled backwards, his face ashen.

The woman tutted angrily. "What is it, man?"

When the attendant didn't reply, she went to his side. And stared. The syringe fell to the floor with a clatter.

"In the name of all that's holy!"

And then Alfie saw them too: fingers of inky cloud emerging from the folds of Selena's dress, coiling around her arms, legs and throat as though some sort of shadow beast had stirred from hibernation to find a juicy morsel in its grasp. Looking up to the observation chamber, Selena saw Alfie's face through the glass. She let forth a piercing scream.

"Help me!" she screamed. "Please God someone help me!"

But Alfie stood motionless, feet rooted to the ground, transfixed by the black cloud that was mutating and growing before him, lengthening shadows of sharp teeth and claws, the sense of a head thrown back, jaws gaping triumphantly. No shape held for more than a second as the darkness continued to billow from the shrieking Selena Marbury, enveloping the attendants and the nurse until it threatened to blot out the room completely.

Elsie staggered over to the door and tried to wrench it open. It rattled on the hinges, apparently stuck fast.

"Please!" she moaned. "For the love of God, let me out!"

From within the cloud, there came the sound of a high-pitched, agonized scream. For a moment Alfie thought it was Selena, but then an attendant's head appeared above the sea of black, waving his arm like a drowning man. His eyes were vacant with terror, and he pawed helplessly at the air as the cloud swallowed him up. Elsie dropped to her knees, clasping her hands together and babbling the Lord's Prayer to herself. It was the last thing Alfie saw before the observation window was filled with a bulging, insatiable black.

His limbs finally unfreezing, Alfie sprinted out of the observation chamber, down the spiral staircase and into the other branch of the passageway, which led to the surgery door. The cries from within the blacked-out room had mingled into a single excruciating screech. Alfie pulled on the door handle with all his strength, but it felt like it had been nailed shut.

Then, looking down at his feet, he saw a small trickle of red liquid seep out from underneath the door. He backed away, a tide of churning bile rising in his throat. Screams were still ringing in his head – whether fresh or simply echoes of earlier horrors, he couldn't tell. Alfie watched with horror, unable to breathe, as the blood crept towards him. Drop by drop, it edged across the flagstones, until finally it brushed against his shoe.

Alfie turned and fled up the steps as though his life depended upon it.

CHAPTER TWENTY

DARKNESS

"Wake up."

Alfie stirred reluctantly, desperately clinging to the last threads of unconsciousness. He was stretched out upon the divan in Dr Grenfell's study, the blinds drawn once more across the window, but there was no sign of any swinging pocket watches, mesmerizing with their gleaming arcs. The doctor was a distant silhouette behind his desk, cloaked in the gloom.

"What am I doing here?" asked Alfie.

"We found you in the Main Hall last night," Grenfell replied. "You'd fainted."

"I don't remember—"

And then Alfie did remember.

"Oh God, Selena!"

He began to cry uncontrollably, his shoulders racked with sobs. His best friend in the world – his love, he had realized only recently – was dead, swallowed up in a cloud of pure nightmare. Never again would he see Selena's wicked smile, or hear her gleeful laugh. Never again would he see her pale, beautiful face. At that moment the world seemed so impossibly cruel and bleak that Alfie wished for the darkness to overwhelm him once more, and leave him unconscious.

Dr Grenfell made no move to comfort Alfie as he sobbed. Instead he rose from his chair and walked over to a table by the window, where he clumsily poured himself a large glass of whiskey, splashing the lacquered surface with spirits.

"What happened last night?" he asked, without looking over his shoulder.

"I found a key to the door Below Stairs," Alfie replied falteringly. "I knew that Selena was down there, and I wanted to make sure she was safe. I was worried. But when I found her, in the surgery. . ." He choked back a sob. "Black smoke was pouring out of her, attacking her. It was attacking all of them. Even when I couldn't see anything, I could hear them. I could hear them screaming."

"I see."

"You don't see!" Alfie said, tears streaming down his cheeks. "Selena asked me to help her! She said that there was something wrong with this place. She was my friend and she asked me to help her but all I could do was *watch*. Just like at the Governor's Ball! And now she's dead!"

"Well, thank you so much for your help, Mandeville," Dr Grenfell replied with brutal sarcasm. "When the Viceroy inquires as to how his daughter ended up dead in my care, I'll tell him that she was butchered by a large black cloud. He will be mollified, I'm sure."

"But I'm telling you the truth!" Alfie protested, sitting up. "I was going to talk to you sooner, really I was, but I was worried you'd think I was mad. There are these creatures – Scrapers – they swim through the floorboards, looking for a fiend that's hiding here. They're the ones who took Perkins, I swear. Ask Yardley!"

Grenfell laughed incredulously. "Ask Yardley?" he echoed. "Take the word of an arsonist and murderer as he spouts gobbledegook about the spirit world? You're all the same: you, the Marbury girl, William Travers ... a rabble of lunatics and killers. You think you're different because your parents are wealthy, but you're just as mad as the wretches in the asylums."

"I'm not mad!"

"When you first arrived at Scarbrook I thought so too. Upon reading your father's letter I felt sure that *he* was the one who needed medical attention, not you. His words made no sense to a man of science. On the other hand, Lord Mandeville was not to be my patient. And what easier way to earn money than to cure a healthy boy of an illness that didn't exist? Yet as I studied you I began to wonder whether there might be a kernel of truth in your father's letter, and I felt a tide of excitement rise up within me. Imagine if I could cure you! My reputation would be redeemed at a stroke!" He shook his head. "It was an act of arrogant folly. Grenfell's folly."

"Why are you saying all this?" pleaded Alfie. "I have only ever obeyed your instructions."

"Of course you have," the doctor said scornfully.

"Poor little Master Mandeville, so harshly treated by those around him. Maybe I'm this fiend these magical creatures are searching for. Or was it Selena, hmm? What do you think?"

"Selena was innocent," replied Alfie, through gritted teeth. "She was the one who was attacked – first in Calcutta, and then Below Stairs. I *know* the fiend is still out there, which means the Scrapers are too. Don't you see? Nobody's safe!"

The doctor knocked back the rest of his whiskey in one gulp and rose unsteadily to his feet. "You're damned right nobody's safe," he said thickly. "But I'll take care of that. Maybe your father was right after all. We'll see what Lord Mandeville makes of your twisted fairy tales after I've written to him and informed him what's occurred here."

As he loomed over the divan, Grenfell reached into his pocket and pulled out a rag. He pressed it against Alfie's face, immersing him in a sickly-sweet odour. Alfie tried to fight him off, but he was powerless in the doctor's strong grip. Soon it felt like Alfie's limbs were drenched in thick treacle, and then his head felt heavy, and darkness washed over him.

Waking up this time was even worse than before. The drug had given Alfie terrible, fevered dreams. He watched from behind the banyan tree as Selena was mesmerized by Travers, who grinned devilishly as he whispered into her ear. He opened the observation curtain in the surgery to find his mother and father strapped down together on the operating table, screaming as the black cloud devoured them. He sat cold and alone on his bed in Chelsea as Scrapers circled around him like sharks, waiting for him to fall into their clutches.

And then Alfie's eyes snapped open. He was lying on a bed in total darkness. Metal bedsprings cut into his back through a smelly mattress. The cold air in the room sent shivers of gooseflesh running across his skin. It felt as though he were lying in a morgue.

As Alfie rolled over with a groan, he heard an object fall from his pocket on to the floor. Wincing at the pain in his head, Alfie got down on his hands and knees to search for it. The flagstones beneath his hands were ice cold to the touch. After a few moments of blind scrabbling, Alfie's fingers closed around a small waxy cylinder. It was the stubby candle from his bedside, which meant the match should also be in his pocket. Alfie offered up a silent prayer of thanks. It was a good job Grenfell hadn't searched him or he would have been condemned to the darkness for God knew how long.

Alfie retrieved the slender match from his pocket. He only had one chance to strike it – best make it count. He stood up and edged towards where he guessed the wall was, his hands outstretched. There was a bad smell in the room that reminded Alfie of the stables his father had taken him to in Calcutta. When his hands bumped up against the wall, he sought out the roughest section of plaster, where the surface was pitted and rutted. Alfie took a deep breath. If this failed, he would be stumbling around blindly for ever. Alfie offered up a quick prayer, closed his eyes, and ran the match up the wall.

The match fizzed angrily into life, a brilliant, blessed spark of light. Crying aloud with triumph, Alfie carefully brought it over to the candle in his other hand and lit the wick. The flame took hold at once, burning with reassuring stillness and strength. A small pool of light surrounded Alfie like a halo. He shook out the match, held up the candle and took in his surroundings for the first time.

He was in a small, windowless room, with high walls that slipped into shadow long before Alfie could make out the ceiling. The only way out of the room appeared to be through a thick iron door set into the wall, but a cursory inspection revealed that it was bolted shut on the other side. But all of this paled into insignificance beside the writing on the walls.

As Alfie looked around the room, he saw that every inch of space was taken up with words and pictures. Some had been drawn in what looked like charcoal; others were etched into the plaster. Red smears of blood and sickly streaks of urine caked the walls. There were violent doodles, daubings of children with no eyes, of horned devil's faces and giant black clouds swallowing everything up. There were frenzied commentaries, as though the writers were speaking aloud:

*SO LOUD PLEASE STOP TOO LOUD
I CAN'T THINK PLEASE STOP*

*Good good good bad good good bad good good good
bad good*

If Mr Punch says he'll behave, may I please be excused?

There were angry threats and promises of violence and,
everywhere, desperate pleas for help. The room felt like
it was filled with a silent chorus of screams.

He was in a cell Below Stairs.

Alfie sat back down on the cot, his brain aching as
he tried to think. He was locked in, with no immediate
hope of getting out of the cell. The candle would only
burn for so long, and then what? He would be plunged
back in the dark. But Alfie had to be strong. He couldn't
give up. Someone would come for him, he told himself.
Dr Grenfell would sober up and realize he had made
a terrible mistake. Travers would find his friend missing
and start to ask questions. Lord Mandeville would pay
a surprise visit to Scarbrook and demand to know his
son's whereabouts.

As Alfie sat quietly, the realization dawned that he
had missed something during his exploration of the cell.
Something very important indeed.

He wasn't alone.

The candlelight wavered as Alfie's hand began to
tremble. He had been so intent on finding out where

he was that he hadn't sensed the presence of another figure in the darkness. They were standing silently in the far corner of the cell, out of the candle's reach. How long had they been still like that? All the while Alfie had been unconscious? Why had they not spoken?

Alfie ran his tongue over his bone-dry lips. "Hello," he said, trying to keep his voice level and calm. "Who are you?"

The figure said nothing.

"I'm sorry I'm in your room," said Alfie, slowly standing up from the bed. "I was put here by mistake. It's all a terrible misunderstanding."

He moved slowly towards the figure in the corner, careful not to make any sudden moves. A thin dribble of wax ran down the side of the candle and set upon his knuckles. Alfie didn't even notice. He could hear the other patient breathing softly, but they made no movement as he neared. Slowly the light revealed him: first a pair of scuffed shoes, then a ragged pair of trousers, then a grimy shirt and waistcoat. As Alfie tentatively lifted up his candle, a face emerged from the darkness. A cry caught in Alfie's throat. His heart sinking, he realized why Dr Grenfell had put him in this cell.

"Got you," said Silas Rothermere, and blew out the candle.

CHAPTER TWENTY-ONE

INTO HELL

They fought viciously, like cornered animals, using fists and elbows, knees and nails. Alfie's was a battle of self-preservation, all the while trying to keep distance between himself and his lumbering assailant. He felt the draught from one of Rothermere's haymakers as his fist swept through the darkness, missing Alfie's face by inches. In response Alfie kicked out, catching Rothermere in the kneecap. The other boy grunted in pain, but didn't stop coming at him.

Alfie tried to duck away once more, only to bang his shins on the metal cot. Another fist swung through the night like a pendulum, this time catching Alfie on the temple. He went sprawling on to the bed, and Rothermere was on him like a flash, driving a knee into his gut. Tears of pain sprang to Alfie's eyes. He tried to push Rothermere off him, but there wasn't the strength in his arms to shift the great weight. As he sensed Rothermere pulling back his arm to hit him again, Alfie realized that he would die here, on this mouldy mattress, in the darkness below the ground.

The punch, when it landed, hurt him less than he had expected, absorbed by the adrenaline coursing through Alfie's system. But then Rothermere was just getting started. As he took another punishing blow, Alfie heard a key rattle in the lock and the door creak open. Light spilled into the room, but Rothermere seemed too intent on pummelling Alfie to notice. Then there was a sickeningly loud thwack, and Rothermere toppled like a felled tree on top of him. A hand pulled the dazed Alfie free.

"Come on," Maria said. "Let's go."

Alfie stumbled to his feet and reeled out into the corridor, the low lamplight dazzling his eyes. His face was damp with blood, his temple pounding where Rothermere had caught him. He winced when Maria slammed the cell door shut and turned the key in the lock. In her other hand was a cricket bat. Noting his startled gaze, she shrugged.

"It was the closest thing I could find to a weapon," she explained, dropping the bat on the floor. "Shall we get out of here?"

They hurried along the corridor to the backdrop of hoots and cries from the other inmates, who'd been stirred into a frenzy by the activity in Rothermere's cell. Images of Selena in the operating room flooded Alfie's mind, and he stumbled out from Below Stairs through a mist of tears. Only at the top of the stairwell did he finally come to a stop, slumping down against the iron railings.

"You're hurt," Maria said, giving his face a critical inspection.

"I'd be hurt a good deal worse if it wasn't for you," Alfie said weakly. "Why did Dr Grenfell put me in a cell? I didn't do anything wrong!"

"I know that. The doctor is angry and needs somebody to blame. He's not thinking clearly. When the staff heard about Selena's death, they packed their bags and fled."

"But Rothermere would have killed me!"

"You have no idea what Scarbrook has been like these past few hours," Maria said grimly. "When they heard about Selena's death, the staff packed their bags and fled. Dr Grenfell persuaded a couple of attendants to lock you up but they left soon afterwards. Now there's no one left apart from me and Dr Grenfell, and he's been drinking in his study all day, probably wondering how he's going to tell the Viceroy his only daughter's dead. How else do you think I was able to get the Below Stairs keys again?"

"What are the patients doing?"

"Whatever takes their fancy, I would imagine. No one's in charge here any more." She paused. "I heard Yardley's tale. About the Scrapers, and this fiend they're hunting. Can it really be true?"

Alfie faltered. "I don't know," he admitted quietly. "But the things I have seen at Scarbrook . . . the things I saw last night . . . were not of this world." He looked down at the ground. "Dr Grenfell suggested that it might have been the fiend who possessed Selena."

"And do you think that, Alfie?"

He shook his head wearily.

"Of course you don't," Maria said urgently. "Selena was a troubled girl, that's for certain, and something dark had preyed upon her. But do you really think she was a creature of pure evil? Come on, Alfie, open your eyes. You know who the fiend is."

"I don't!"

"That's why I left the photograph under your pillow."

"That was you? But why?"

"I needed you to see, Alfie. You can't hide from this any longer. There are patients here who are sick, and there are patients here who are healthy. But there's only one patient here who is cruel. Who takes pleasure from bullying and hurting people." Maria rolled up her sleeve, revealing a dark mass of bruises. "Who would do *this* to a girl he claimed he cared for. Whose idea of love is closer to hate than any normal person could comprehend."

"Maria, you can't mean—"

"It's William, Alfie. William Travers is the fiend. Admit it!"

He couldn't. It was his friend she was talking about. She had to be wrong. But then a series of images ran through Alfie's head: Harker's coffin, and the look of hatred upon the boy's face in the photograph; Lucy fleeing in tears from the game of blind man's buff; the manipulated Rothermere, itching to hurt Alfie. In the short time that he had known Travers, Alfie had seen supposed friends and loved ones mocked, hurt and betrayed. Of course Travers was the fiend. Deep down, he had known it all along.

"Maybe you're right," he said slowly. "Maybe it *is* Travers the Scrapers are looking for. But whatever he's done, he's still my friend. I can't just abandon him."

A faint smile touched Maria's face. "You're a nice boy," she murmured. "Too nice for this horrible place. And certainly too nice for Travers."

Alfie rubbed a hand wearily across his forehead. He felt more tired than ever, too tired to argue with Maria. She took his hand and said softly:

"It won't end until the Scrapers get what they want."

"I can't just give them Travers!" Alfie protested.

"Then convince him to leave. If he thinks he can outrun his demons, let him try." Maria turned Alfie's face towards hers. "But know this to be true – if William Travers stays at Scarbrook for even one more night, then more innocent people will die. Do you think these things will just stop and go away?"

The deepening dusk had turned the corridor a murky grey colour. It would not be long before Scarbrook was clutched in night's embrace. Rising from their seats by the railing, they walked slowly through the sanatorium, Maria's footfalls catlike in the quiet. As they neared the library, Alfie became aware of a commotion coming from the other side of the door. He frowned.

"What's going on in there?"

"I've no idea," Maria replied. "It was empty when last I passed."

They both flinched at the sound of Travers' voice booming out from within.

"Well, it isn't empty any more." Alfie took the girl's hands in his. "Go to your room and lock your door now, Maria. The further away you are from him, the better."

"Be careful, Alfie."

Maria burrowed her head against his neck, kissing him softly, and then hurried away in the direction of the servants' rooms. Alfie waited until she had vanished into the gloom before pushing open the library door.

The sudden blast of heat made him take a step back. A raging fire had been built up in the hearth, filling the library with suffocating waves of smoke that billowed out into the hallway. Patients were running amok around the bookshelves, their clothes dishevelled and their faces streaked with soot. With the scuttle lying empty by the hearth, they were flinging books into the fire to build it up, adding the crackle of paper to the spit of coals and the roar of flames. Shadows danced giddy reels across the wooden panels on the walls behind them.

In the centre of the room stood William Travers. He was brandishing a poker like a broadsword, his white shirt soaked through with sweat. Throwing back his head, he roared with satisfaction.

"Stoke up the fire!" Travers bellowed. "If he wants Hell, let's give it to him!"

As he edged inside the library, Alfie saw that Yardley

was lying at Travers' feet, curled up into a protective ball. The other patients circled him like wild animals, jeering loudly and pushing him back every time he tried to stand. Catherine was cowering in the corner of the room, her horrified gaze fixed upon the fire, seemingly too terrified to help her brother.

Travers leaned over Yardley and jabbed him in the side with his poker. "Everything was fine until you started telling your little ghost stories," he seethed. "And now look what's happening! I think it's *you* these things are after. You look pretty damn fiendish to me. Remember it was your sister who found Perkins' eyes – did you tell her where to look?"

Yardley cowered as the circle tightened around him. To Alfie's eyes, stinging in the smoke, the patients seemed to shift in form – one minute cackling hyenas, the next snakes, hissing with delight. Closer and closer they slithered, with flickering, malicious tongues. . .

"Leave him alone!" Alfie cried, elbowing his way to Yardley's side.

"Ah, Mandeville!" There was the barest gleam of recognition in Travers' manic eyes. "You're just in time. I'm going to ram this poker down the little piglet's throat and roast him upon the fire."

"Travers!" gasped Alfie. "Have you gone mad?"

"Under the circumstances, I'd call this entirely sane. I'll not be called a madman for protecting myself."

"Look at you all!" Alfie cried, turning to the other patients, who had paused in surprise at his interruption.

"Will you let him talk you into murder just like that? What's happened to you?"

"Don't listen to him!" Travers shouted. "You saw him in the church. He's as crazy as Yardley!"

But a sudden element of doubt had been introduced into the room like a cooling breeze. A girl hesitated in the act of throwing another book on to the fire, sheepishly returning it to the shelf; a boy blinked and stopped kicking Yardley. It was as though Alfie's arrival had broken some kind of spell.

"You're listening to Mandeville?" said Travers, disbelievingly. "Can't you see that this is the only course of action left to us?"

He searched the patients' faces for agreement, but no one would hold his gaze. Alfie folded his arms. With a snarl, Travers hurled the poker into the fire and stormed out of the room, knocking Sampson to the ground on his way past.

Alfie knelt down beside Yardley. Blood trickled from a cut on the boy's lip, and there was a nasty bruise on his cheek.

"You stopped him!" he whispered.

Alfie smiled sympathetically. "Are you all right?"

Yardley nodded. "I can't help Travers," he said hoarsely. "His eyes are blind to the danger he's in."

"I know," said Alfie.

He gently helped Yardley to his feet. The boy scurried away without a word of thanks, grabbing his sister's hand and dragging her away from the fire and out of the room. Alfie turned to find the rest of the room staring at him.

"Well don't just stand there gawping!" Alfie shouted with exasperation. "For God's sake, someone dampen down that fire, or you'll burn the rest of this bloody building down around our ears. And if you've got any sense you'll get to bed before night falls and the Scrapers come looking for you!"

He hastened from the library, grateful to escape the inferno. His shirt was plastered to his skin, and the smoke had made his wounds sting. The stewed summer air in the corridors felt like an ice bath in comparison.

It didn't take long to locate Travers. Alfie found him sitting on the bottom step of the staircase in the Main Hall, forlornly rubbing a scuff on his shoe. Travers' hair was plastered to his forehead with sweat, and there seemed something deflated about his manner, as though an inner fire had been extinguished. He barely looked up as Alfie approached and cautiously sat down beside him. They sat in silence for a long time before Travers eventually cleared his throat.

"Bad form again, I take it?" he asked lightly.

"I think it's a little worse than that."

"Ah."

There was another lengthy pause, and this time it was Alfie who spoke up.

"This can't go on, William," he said. "Surely you must see that."

Travers nodded. He grabbed a fistful of his dark

hair and tugged at it fiercely. "It's just that there's this *darkness* . . . this infernal darkness that clouds my mind and grips my heart. I tried to remove it, to dig it out from inside of me, but it remains there, festering like a canker, twisting and spoiling everything I do and feel until it is black and rotten."

"You need help," Alfie said. "You're not safe here."

"Of course," laughed Travers humourlessly. "Your and Yardley's beloved Scrapers. Coming for their fiend. Well, if it's me they're after, they can bloody well take me!"

"You must get away from here!" Alfie urged. "Board a steamer to America or East Asia. Live up a mountain. Just get as far away as possible."

Travers smiled weakly. "You want me to try and outrun Hell?"

"What else can you do?"

Travers toyed with a shoelace. "I hear the Bahamas are quite pleasant at this time of year," he said eventually. "I could gain passage on one of my father's ships."

"That's more like it!" said Alfie, with what he hoped was an encouraging smile. "You could write to me when you get there." Patting his friend on the back, he climbed to his feet.

Travers gave him an inquiring glance. "And whilst I'm making travel plans, where might you be headed?"

"Dr Grenfell's study," Alfie replied. "I think he was going to write a letter to my father about me, but Maria told me he'd been drinking all day. Maybe it's still there."

Travers raised an eyebrow. "Planning a burglary, Master Mandeville?"

"If needs be. If my father reads that letter, as soon as Scarbrook is closed down I'll only be locked up somewhere worse. I've had my fill of these places for one lifetime."

Briskly brushing his trousers clean, Travers hauled himself up from the staircase. "I'll come with you," he declared, with a hint of his old insouciance. "One final sally forth, for old time's sake. Never let it be said that William Travers is not a team player."

Alfie hid a grimace. With the onset of night and the threat of the Scrapers abroad, the last thing he wanted was Travers by his side, but neither did he feel able to turn down his tormented friend's offer of help. He couldn't snub him now. Even so, as they left the Main Hall, Alfie had to stop himself from breaking into a run, and he tensed at the slightest noise. Upon reaching Dr Grenfell's study, he found the door ajar, and slipped gratefully inside. The blinds had been lifted, allowing the rising moon to illuminate the room. The milky glow caught and played on a coating of shattered glass across the carpet. Judging by the cloying stench of alcohol and the depth and range of the jagged shards, the doctor must have smashed every bottle in his collection.

It had been his last, futile act. Dr Edmund Grenfell, the eminent physician, Scarbrook House's greatest and most passionate champion, lay face down at his desk, a trail of clotted blood leading from an ugly wound in his temple. An antique pistol was lying on the glass on the floor, dropped from his outstretched hand.

As they crept across the glass, their shoes crunching on malicious points and edges, Travers glanced questioningly at a folded piece of paper in Grenfell's right hand.

Stepping over to the doctor's desk, Alfie prised the letter free, shuddering as his fingers brushed against the corpse's. He moved over to the window, unfolded the paper and began to read by moonlight.

"That the one?" hissed Travers.

Alfie shook his head. "No," he said softly, with a frown. "This is the letter my father wrote to Dr Grenfell, the one I gave him when I first came here. It—"

He stopped speaking.

CHAPTER TWENTY-TWO

A FATHER'S LAMENT

Chelsea, 14 July 1897

To Doctor Edmund Grenfell
Scarbrook House
Hertfordshire

Sir,

*These words do not flow easily from my pen. My entire
life has been spent in command, whether striving for the
increase of the Mandeville fortune or in the name of Her
Majesty, bringing new territories under the blessed aegis
of our Empire. Humility does not come naturally to me,
nor does my knee bend readily in supplication. But I can
no longer deny that I have reached my wits' end. In utter
desperation, I find myself writing this letter to beg – beg,
Dr Grenfell – for your assistance.*

*The seeds of my desolation were sown many years ago,
during the most joyous occurrence of my life: the birth of our
son, Alfred. Lady Mandeville had endured two previous*

227

pregnancies that had ended prematurely, and the doctors believed she was incapable of bringing a child into the world. I had given up hope of ever seeing my family's proud line continue. So you cannot begin to imagine my delight when my wife conceived anew, and this time the baby proved hardier than his predecessors. It seemed that my long nights of prayer had been answered. Both mother and son survived the birth, and the sight of my tiny boy sleeping peacefully in his cradle afterwards brought a lump to my throat and a tear to my eye. With our family now complete, the Mandevilles could look forward to a long and happy life together.

Alfred, it appeared, had other ideas.

Even as a small child, he proved himself capable of small, wanton acts of cruelty – the taunting and torturing of insects and animals; the stealing of servants' trinkets and keepsakes; the pinching and biting of other, smaller infants. At first I put it down to mere youthful excess, and tried to correct Alfred's behaviour in the usual manner, with hand and cane. I did not see – did not want to see? – the permanent defect in our son's heart: the knot in the wood; the flaw in the glasswork.

An incident soon after Alfred's twelfth birthday brutally tore the blindfold from my eyes. Whilst taking a turn around the grounds of our country estate in Hampshire, Lady Mandeville stumbled across our child attacking a wounded blackbird in the grounds of our estate. Like some untamed savage, Alfred ripped the stricken creature open with a butter knife, before stuffing the still-pulsating innards into his mouth.

228

I was about to write that you could imagine Lady Mandeville's horror, but on reflection I am not sure that this is true.

It was only then that my wife came forward with a tearful confession. It was only then that I learned the truth about my "son". In her desperation to produce a child, Lady Mandeville had been offering up prayers of her own — but not to any power that God would recognize. I had long been aware of my wife's interest in spiritual matters, but I had thought it a harmless pastime, little more than a childlike fascination with ghosts and fairies. But it was far more serious than that. When my back was turned, Lady Mandeville had been courting dark, unknowable powers in séances, begging the spirit world for a child. It was during one of these unholy gatherings, she told me miserably, that she had felt a stir inside. Within days the doctor confirmed her pregnancy. Lady Mandeville had steeled herself to tell me, but my unconfined joy at the news had promptly silenced her, and kept her that way for over a decade.

I grieve to say that this confession proved a fatal poison in our marriage cup. Try as I might, I could not forgive my wife for her deceit. Consumed by guilt for her child's behaviour, Lady Mandeville drifted more and more into the shades of lethargy. She began taking laudanum for her nerves, but the drug only served to further dull her senses. I fear that one day soon she will go to sleep and never wake up. For his part, Alfred seems unaware that he has torn his own family apart. Nothing disturbs his mask of innocence. Whatever evil lies within him possesses him only sporadically, seemingly without his knowledge.

Following the incident with the blackbird, I sternly chastised Alfred and locked him in his room without food for several days, but the boy's bewildered distress caused my wife so much heartache that we resolved to try a new approach. Hopeful that a change in climate might alleviate Alfred's condition, we moved to India, all the while taking the greatest of pains to ensure that no one became aware of our secret shame – save for our faithful butler Stowbridge, whose complicity was necessary to ensure the household staff's ignorance.

Upon our taking up residence in Calcutta, we harboured hopes that our new surroundings had wrought a positive change in Alfred. Undaunted by the simmering humidity, he took to the alien city like a native. To our delight, he maintained as civil and polite an air as one could wish for – behaving like the true Mandeville we had always hoped he would become. As you will no doubt discover, when he is not suffering from one of his episodes, Alfred is possessed of the sweetest and most good-natured of temperaments.

Then, in December of last year, came the Governor's Ball. God have mercy on us, but it seemed the evil was only sleeping.

It was the social event of the season, for those who cared for that sort of thing. As a man who thrives upon the deal rather than the dance, I stood back and ceded the floor to youth. So when the Viceroy noted that his daughter Selena – a close friend and confidante of Alfred's – had disappeared, it was only natural that I should volunteer to find her. In truth, I was eager to escape the ballroom's forced frivolity.

A cursory tour of the mansion offered no clues to Selena's whereabouts, so I headed out into the gardens. There, beyond the banyan trees, I found her. She was standing in a trance upon the grass, her limbs frozen yet her eyes screaming out for help. Worst of all was the sight of Alfred – my son! My own flesh and blood! – menacing the helpless girl, burning her arm with a smouldering coal whilst he whispered dark, unintelligible words into her ear. Disturbed by my appearance, his head snapped upwards, and he greeted me with a gaze of blank malevolence and a feral snarl. When I commanded him to move away, he released the coal, dropped to all fours and scurried away into the undergrowth, as though he had rejected the most basic tenets of humanity.

I have hunted many wild and dangerous beasts in my time, but nothing had prepared me for the savagery of my own son. In a state of shock, I picked up the dazed Selena and carried her into the house. Upon questioning by the Viceroy, it transpired that she had no recollections of what or who had accosted her. God forgive me, I saw my opportunity. I remembered that Alfred had complained to me of a young Hindoo boy following him and Selena. When I told the Viceroy, a search was hastily organized, and within the hour the punkawallah's son was brought before us. Naturally he pleaded his innocence, but the strength of my word was enough to ensure his conviction. The punkawallah's son was first flogged and then executed, and his family was driven penniless from Calcutta. As a man of honour, it caused me untold shame to bring about the death of a complete innocent, but you must understand, doctor, that this was my son. And a Mandeville to boot!

Stowbridge discovered the true author of the evening's crime later that night, unconscious by the side of the racetrack on the Maidan. As before, Alfred's mind had protected him from the horrific reality of his own actions and even he believed the punkawallah's son to be responsible. We waited for a fortnight before returning to London, slipping into our residence under the cover of midnight like criminals. Inconsolable, my wife and I fell into bitter argument, as though we could solve our cursed son's problems by blaming each other. The atmosphere in our house took on an Arctic chill. When word came to us in May that Selena Marbury was returning to Britain, amid scurrilous rumours concerning her mental health, Alfred developed bouts of sleeplessness. It was a sign of our desperation that we took this as a good omen. After all, was this not the first time that he had shown any recognition of his grave crimes?

We were fools to hope. Blind, idiotic fools. Last night my wife and I returned from the theatre to find the house shrouded in an awful silence, and a trail of blood glistening across the chequered hallway. Bidding Lady Mandeville to wait in the safety of the carriage, I crept into the drawing-room and opened my gun cabinet. Clutching my rifle, I followed the blood trail up the stairs and through the master bedroom doors into Hell. Stowbridge's body had been laid out neatly upon the bed. Our faithful butler had been blinded, his vital organs ripped out and placed into a careful pile on the bedside table. My son was lying peacefully beside the corpse on the bed, soaked in Stowbridge's blood, my South African hunting knife still in his grasp.

Even the battlefields of the Crimea could not have held greater horrors than this sight. I was at once violently ill, and it took me several minutes to compose myself. In a state of manic delirium, I carried the remains downstairs and buried them at the bottom of the garden. Then I cleaned up my drowsy son and returned him to bed. There he has lain for several hours. His mother cannot bring herself to look upon him; I confess to thoughts of murder.

As I sit at my writing desk, the sight of my hunting rifle propped up against the wall makes me wonder whether I am being punished for previous crimes. After all, the apple does not fall far from the tree, and if my son is a murderer then I am also. Frederick Scarbrook's death was not an accident; when the lion charged our hunting party I took careful aim and fired a bullet through the heart of my best friend. I have always been a jealous man, and his friendship with Lady Mandeville was something I could not bear. My wife swears that her heart was ever mine, and that nothing improper occurred between herself and Fred. Even so, I think that day I fatally wounded her as well – only her decline has been a bloodless, brutally drawn-out affair. Perhaps her mental fragility has also required institutionalization, but in truth I cannot bear to be parted from her, not even for a day. I suppose this is the price of love – and of memory, and of regret.

Perhaps our son is too far gone; there may be nothing to be done. Perhaps I should entrust him to a churchman, to drive away the devil that haunts him. Instead I am placing my last, desperate vestiges of faith in you. I am a rich and powerful man, Dr Grenfell, and you can be assured your fortune will be made if you can help Alfred. As I have told you, he appears completely unaware of his terrible crimes, and believes that he is being sent to Scarbrook House merely to cure his sleeplessness. I must insist that you refrain from enlightening him, and that the secrets divulged in this letter remain in the strictest confidence. Upon learning his true nature (or mine, for that matter) who knows the foul depths to which he might descend?

Should you decide in your wisdom to take on Alfred's case, I would ask that you take the greatest of care with him. He is undoubtedly a monster; he is also my son.

I remain, your humble servant,

Lord Richard Mandeville

CHAPTER TWENTY-THREE

BEDTIME

The letter spiralled out of Alfie's grasp. He bent over, coughing up a thin stream of bile on to the carpet.

"Good Lord, Alfie!" Travers exclaimed. "What on earth's the matter?"

Alfie ran over to the window and heaved it open, taking in stuttering lungfuls of the night air. He felt dizzyingly nauseous, and there was a piercing pain in his chest. It had to be a mistake. There was no way. . . He could remember the blackbird as clearly as if it were yesterday, a red mess of innards spilling out on to the grass. How could he have been responsible for that? And for Selena? And Stowbridge?

"*Our faithful butler had been blinded, his vital organs ripped out and placed into a careful pile on the bedside table. . .*"

The thought of it filled his throat with bile once more, and Alfie vomited on to the flower bed outside the window. As he coughed and wiped his mouth with a handkerchief, behind him Travers picked up Lord Mandeville's letter. His brow knitted with concentration as he read.

"Please!" Alfie croaked. "Don't—!"

Travers waved away his protests, finishing the letter in silence before carefully folding it up. He ran a hand through his hair, his expression masked in the gloom.

"Travers?" said Alfie uncertainly.

"Oh, you're good." Travers' voice was deathly soft. "You're very good indeed. You had us all fooled, didn't you? Floating around here with your 'sleep problems' and your innocent little face, like butter wouldn't melt: *Don't be so mean, Travers* and *Don't be so cruel, Travers* and *You're in danger, Travers*. You're so good you nearly had me on a steamer to the West Indies, convinced that I was going to spend the rest of my life being chased by creatures from Hell."

He advanced through the shadows towards Alfie, his footsteps crunching upon the broken glass.

"But it wasn't me, was it?" he whispered. "I'm not the reason the Scrapers are here. You are. You're the fiend!"

"No!" Alfie stumbled backwards. "I swear, I'm not! I can't be!"

Travers jabbed the folded letter into Alfie's chest. "Condemned by your father's own hand. No wonder he couldn't bring himself to write to you. He knew what you were."

"Please, Travers!" Alfie gasped, backing into the wall. "I can't breathe!"

"Your mother wanted a child so much she went looking in Hell for one. Only she got more than she bargained for, didn't she? She begged for a child, and she found a fiend."

Alfie moaned with fear.

"You were born a devil, and you're still a devil," Travers continued remorselessly. "You burned your mark on Selena Marbury in Calcutta and infected her with your evil."

"Selena was my friend!" Alfie cried. "I would never have hurt her. It was Ajay! It was the punkawallah's son!"

"By. Your. Father's. Own. Hand," Travers repeated, through clenched teeth. "You've walked hand in hand with murder and evil wherever you've gone. Your very presence at Harker's funeral caused the dead to rise up in protest. You claim you've got insomnia, but actually it's the other way around, isn't it, Alfie? You've been asleep for a very long time. Now it's time to wake up."

Alfie sank to the floor with a wail, clutching his head in his hands. "It's not true!" he sobbed. "I'm not a fiend!"

"Find another fool to swallow your lies," Travers said darkly, dragging Alfie to his feet. "You'll not be catching me out again."

"W-where are you taking me?"

"I'm going to deliver you to the Scrapers myself. You're going back where you belong!"

"No! Let go of me!"

Trying to wriggle free from Travers' grip, Alfie caught the larger boy with an elbow to the side of the head. Travers grunted in pain, and Alfie drove his shoulder into his gut, sending both of them sprawling on to the divan. Before Alfie could extract himself from the tangle of limbs, Travers had recovered and wrapped his large hands around Alfie's throat. His eyes narrowing with hatred, he began to squeeze. Black clouds mushroomed in front of Alfie's eyes, and his head swam from lack of air. Summoning the last of his strength, he grabbed hold of Travers and rolled him off the divan, sending the two of them tumbling into a sea of broken glass.

A searing pain shot up Alfie's side like a harpoon. Crying out in pain, he pushed himself into a sitting position, ignoring the glass splinters embedding themselves in his palm. As his hands explored his ribs, they came across a shard poking out from his side. Alfie gritted his teeth and yanked the shard from his stomach. Pain threatened to overwhelm him. Gasping in agony, still clutching his side, he hauled himself up on to the divan.

It was only then that he realized that Travers was dying.

The boy was lying prone on the floor, his eyes blinking rapidly with distress. A long sliver of glass was wedged in his throat. He clutched at it forlornly, trying to stem the steady stream of blood ebbing from his body on to the carpet.

"Travers!" Alfie cried. "No!"

A thick bubbling sound escaped from Travers' mouth. Alfie slid back down on to the floor and grabbed his friend's hand.

"I'm sorry," Alfie whispered. "So very sorry."

Travers gurgled feebly, and his body gave out a violent shudder. Then the spasms ceased and his limbs went horribly limp. Two lifeless eyes stared up at the ceiling.

Alfie recoiled in horror. Using the arm of the divan as a support, he climbed to his feet and staggered for the door. This had to be a nightmare. Shortly he'd wake up back in his bed with a shout and Travers would mock him cruelly for being a crybaby, but it would be all right. Anything would be better than this. *But it isn't a nightmare,* said a cruel voice in his head, *because you have to sleep to have a nightmare, and you can't sleep. . .*

Alfie stumbled out of the study holding his side before another wave of pain made him collapse in the corridor beyond, like a shipwreck victim clawing his way to shore. He retched violently, staining his lips with thick red liquid. As he wiped his mouth, Alfie was overwhelmed by a fit of hysterical laughter. He rolled on to his back and laughed and howled and sobbed all at the same time, his side aching with every movement.

A loud scuffing sound cut through his delirium. As Alfie peered down the corridor, the laughter died in his throat. A low-slung shape had emerged from the welling darkness, and was sliding across the floor towards him. The Scrapers had returned. Alfie tried to stand, but his legs collapsed from under him. His stomach felt as though it was on fire. In this condition, there was no way he could make it out of Scarbrook. His only chance of salvation lay upstairs in the dormitory, beneath the blankets on his bed.

He would not let them hunt him down. Not like this. Alfie dragged himself across the floor with renewed determination, leaving a trail of blood smeared across the corridor and the floorboards of the Main Hall. He moved in complete silence, channelling every last drop of energy into keeping ahead of his unholy predator. The Scraper clawed relentlessly after him, face pressed down against the ground, hungrily devouring the gap between them.

By the time Alfie had reached the foot of the main staircase, he could hear the Scraper's jagged breaths behind him, the agitated scratch of its nails upon the floor. He tried to speed up, but every step he pulled himself up only opened the wound in his side further. His shirt was drenched with blood, and his head was dizzy. As Alfie manoeuvred around the left turn of the stairs, a claw snaked out and grabbed his ankle. He twisted round to see the Scraper staring up at him. Alfie screamed with horror.

In stretching out to reach him, the Scraper had lifted its head from the floor, revealing the true horror of its being. It wasn't swimming through the floor. It was a half man: possessing only half a head, half a body, one leg and one arm. It looked as though it had been sliced in two down the middle. Where the left-hand side of its head should have been, there was nothing but a pulsing mass of veins and arteries where its face came to a premature end.

Instinctively Alfie lashed out, his foot making a shuddering connection with the Scraper's jaw. The creature made a mangled sound of pain and let go of his ankle. Redoubling his efforts, Alfie frantically clawed his way to the top of the steps, but there was no respite for him on the landing. The door to the girls' room opened, and a second Scraper appeared, snarling with recognition at the sight of him. Alfie dragged himself along the landing, keeping his eyes fixed on the looming boys' dormitory rather than the two grimacing creatures on his tail. When the door drew within reach, Alfie reached up and twisted the knob, ignoring the stabbing pain in his side. The door fell open, and he tumbled inside.

He found the dormitory steeped in fear. Terrified moans greeted his entrance, and the boys sank deeper beneath their quivering blankets, not daring a glance towards the doorway. Scanning the room, Alfie could have sobbed with relief. There was no sign of any other Scrapers. He crawled across the floor, past Sampson's bed, and Brooke's, and Yardley's. Alfie only had eyes for his own bed. He didn't need to look behind him to know that the Scrapers had clawed their way into the room – the sobs and whimpers from the other patients told him all he needed to know. Too late, Alfie realized that he could have climbed into Travers' empty bed. But even that didn't matter, for his own was now within touching distance. The Scrapers would have to come for him another time. Reaching up to pull himself on to the bed, Alfie felt his fingers close triumphantly over his blanket.

There was a movement in the yawning blackness beneath his bed. An eye blinked; a gnarled hand reached out and tore the blanket from Alfie's grasp. Half a mouth twisted into half a smile.

"No!" whimpered Alfie. "Please God, no!"

The Scraper lunged out from the gloom, digging jagged nails into Alfie's arms as it enveloped him in a fetid embrace. Over by Travers' bed, there came two hoarse wheezes of triumph as the other Scrapers closed in on their prey. The floor beneath them began to char and smoulder, the floorboards suddenly burning hot to the touch. Alfie tried desperately to break free, but he was engulfed in Scrapers now, their lank hair slapping against his skin as they pinned him to the ground. His skin screamed with pain as the floorboards caught fire; his eyes wept in the billowing black smoke.

"Welcome home," a voice hissed in his ear.

With a cavernous groan, the floor gave way beneath them, and Alfie fell into the smoky darkness.

CHAPTER TWENTY-FOUR

FAREWELL

The morning found Scarbrook House in a state of fragile watchfulness. The kitchen fireplaces lay dormant, the tables in the dining room still cluttered with the plates and glasses of the previous day's lunch. No footsteps creaked upon the stairs; no voices exclaimed in the corridor. Outside, in the grounds, the chirping of a blackbird sounded violent in the quiet. Unnerved by the silence, the bird suddenly took off from its branch and disappeared into the sky amid a flutter of wings.

Up in the boys' dormitory, by the bed nearest the window, a large hole with blackened edges had been burned into the floorboards, and through the floors directly below – all the way down to the cellar – before plunging on deep into the earth. It looked as though the sanatorium had been struck by a plummeting comet.

A small group of patients had clustered around the hole, peering fearfully into the dizzying, all-enveloping dark. They gasped and giggled, skittish horses in a thunderstorm, their mood teetering between terror and hysterical amusement.

"I wonder how far it descends?" asked Brooke, a nervous voice from the back of the group.

"Why don't you jump down it and see?" Sampson replied quickly.

"Ha ha. I'm just saying, it looks like it goes on for miles."

"Did the Scrapers really come again last night?" Lucy Albright piped up tremulously. She was gnawing on her lip so fervently her mouth was tinged with blood. "And took Alfie?"

The boys nodded, their silence an eloquent expression of a shared, unspoken horror.

"I tried to warn him," said Yardley, his saucer eyes damp with melancholy. His sister was hanging back behind him, her arms wrapped protectively around her doll. "I told him that fire awaited. But he didn't listen to me. No one ever does."

Sampson ran a hand through his hair. "You really think that goes all the way down?" His voice dropped to a whisper. "*To Hell?*"

"Not any more," replied Yardley. "They don't keep the gates open for long. Pray it's the closest you ever get."

"The Scrapers are gone, though?" Lucy asked. "We're safe?"

"I suppose."

"What about Travers?" asked Sampson. "What happened to him?"

"He's dead," a voice replied from the doorway.

Maria was dressed for travel, in a thick brown overcoat and boots, her possessions stored in a bulky carpetbag. "I found his body in Grenfell's study. The doctor's dead, too."

Lucy put a hand over her mouth and began to sob.

"Save your tears, girl," Maria said briskly. "William Travers could not live easily in this world. Perhaps his soul will find rest elsewhere."

She glanced towards the dark hole in the corner of the room.

"The rumours are true?" she asked Yardley. "It was Alfie?"

He nodded sadly.

"The poor boy," said Maria, crossing her chest. "The fiend must have burrowed deep into his soul. It had found the perfect place to hide – the body of a true innocent. Imagine the horror of discovering that the devil lay inside you."

Her words had a sobering effect on the patients, who turned and shuffled towards the door, unwilling to keep their backs to the hole for a second longer than necessary. Only Yardley and Catherine remained to watch as Maria produced a key upon a chain from around her neck, knelt down by Travers' bedside table and unlocked the drawer. She reached inside and pulled out a carved wooden box, flicking up the catch. As she opened the box, Yardley caught sight of the telltale glitter of silver and gold. Maria smiled.

"I hope you can see me, William," she whispered.

"Your thieving magpie found your key and has your precious valuables. They're mine now."

She looked up to give Yardley and Catherine a challenging gaze. "I'm taking this as a gift from William to me. The way he treated me, he owed me this much. Do you disagree?"

"It's no business of ours," replied Yardley, with a shrug. "What will you do with it?"

"Get as far away from here as possible. Start again. You should do the same."

Yardley let out a reedy laugh. "And go where?" he said. "Our parents are dead; the rest of our family have disowned us. Scarbrook may be cursed, but then so is the rest of the world for us. Someone will come soon enough. We will not be abandoned."

As Maria stuffed Travers' box inside her carpetbag, Catherine stared at Yardley and pointedly folded her arms. He started, and hurriedly handed Maria a piece of paper.

"I nearly forgot – my sister found this amongst the piano music," explained Yardley. "She thought you might want it."

Maria's eyes widened in surprise. The wrinkled paper had been torn from a book of lullabies, and contained the lyrics to a song she knew all too well.

"'My Lady Wind'!" she exclaimed. "Alfie and I could never remember the lyrics! How did Catherine know?"

Yardley shrugged. "She may be mute, but her eyes

and ears work just as well as ours. She heard you talking about it in the library."

Maria looked down at the silent girl and smiled. "Thank you." She folded up the paper and slipped it in her pocket. "Good luck to you both. May Hell never touch your lives again."

"The spirit world will protect us," said Yardley, taking his sister's small hand in his. "It always does."

As Maria walked out of the dormitory, a gust of hot, stale air, like dragon's breath, flew out from the hole, the long exhalation of a hunger finally satisfied. For the final time she walked along the landing and down the staircase into the Main Hall. Finding herself suddenly eager for the fresh air, her footsteps quickened, until Maria was almost running for Scarbrook's front entrance, and then she had crossed the threshold and was standing outside, blinking in the bright sunlight.

"My lady wind, my lady wind,
Went round about the house to find
A chink to get her foot in, her foot in."

As she walked down the hill towards the front gate, the lullaby's words took Maria back to her time in the workhouse – the endless hours spent spinning and weaving, until her fingers were red-raw; the freezing chill in the bedroom as the night-time took hold; Alice's kind embrace, her soft voice hushing Maria to sleep. Comforting memories, in a strange sort of way. The workhouse had been a hard, bleak place, with more than its fair share of miseries, but the only devils there had been the overseers, and at least they were flesh and blood.

Travers' valuables were rattling loudly in the box inside her carpetbag. Maria couldn't help wondering at the size of fortune she was now carrying. One that could provide her with many years of comfort, she didn't doubt. Perhaps she could try and track down Alice, and repay the kindness the elder girl had shown her all those years ago. For the first time she could remember, Maria dared to hope about the future.

As she dreamed of a happier life, ahead of her a carriage appeared at the entrance gates.

> *"She tried the keyhole in the door,*
> *"She tried the crevice in the floor,*
> *"and drove the chimney soot in, the soot in."*

The carriage was moving at great speed, the horses whinnying in protest at the repeated crack of the coachman's whip. As Maria stepped on to the grass to let it past, it skidded to a halt on the path. A coarse-faced coachman leaned down from his seat and jerked his head in the direction of the sanatorium.

"You work there?"

Maria nodded.

"I've come from the village," he said. "Is it true Grenfell's dead?"

"I'm afraid so."

"So who's in charge, then?"

"No one."

"I knew it!" said the coachman, through clenched teeth. "Can sense trouble from a mile away, I can. Knew it even before word reached Almsworth. That's why his Lordship hired me – the brother of the late Lord Derbyshire, I mean. He pays me to keep watch over the place, in case the boy who sets fire to things escapes."

"You mean Yardley?"

The man nodded grimly. "Woe betide those near him if he gets free. He loves a flame the way a sailor loves a drink. I'm to get the boy somewhere where he can't harm anyone – by force, if needs be."

"I left him up in the house not five minutes ago," said Maria, shielding her eyes from the sun. "With Catherine."

The coachman frowned. "Who?

"And then one night when it was dark,
"She blew up such a tiny spark
"That all the town was bothered. . ."

"Catherine!" Maria replied. "The mute girl?"

"I'm only here for the boy," the coachman said firmly, "I've no room for other passengers."

"But she's his sister!"

"Sister?" The coachman let out a grizzled bark of laughter. "Hah!" That's a good one. Yardley's sister has been dead over a year now."

"Dead?" gasped Maria. "That's impossible!"

"Heard it from his Lordship's own mouth, as clear as we are talking now," the coachman retorted. "The girl died in the same fire that killed her parents. So unless Yardley's been walking round with a ghost, you've been seeing things." He leaned forward with a leering smile. "You sure you work up there, or were you locked up with the rest of the lunatics?"

Maria stared at him in astonishment.

"From it she raised such flame and smoke
"That many in great terror woke,
"And many more were smothered. . ."

Before she could reply, the coachman snarled and cracked his whip, and the carriage flew on up the hillside. Maria looked back towards Scarbrook, its wounded remains still sitting proudly on the crest. Could it really be true? Were the other patients in danger? Should she go back?

It was the past, someone else's tale to tell now. She wanted no part of it.

Turning her back on the sanatorium, Maria walked down the path and out through the gates towards Almsworth. Behind her a tendril of black smoke rose up into the air from the west wing of Scarbrook House like a bleak beacon of defiance, or a mournful gesture of farewell.